W9-DBZ-010

"Who was he?" Linda asked.

"A Cuban agent." Carter knelt and searched through the agent's clothing.

"You must be a spy," the girl decided.

"Must be," Carter echoed.

He found the tiny black dot between the first and second toes of the left foot. He took an addressed envelope from his pocket, stuck the dot in the upper-right corner, licked a stamp, and put it over the microdot.

"Wow!" the girl said. "You really *are* a spy!"

"We'd better get out of here," Carter said.

NICK CARTER IS IT!

"Nick Carter out-Bonds James Bond."
–Buffalo Evening News

"Nick Carter is America's #1 espionage agent."
–Variety

"Nick Carter is razor-sharp suspense."
–King Features

"Nick Carter is extraordinarily big."
–Bestsellers

"Nick Carter has attracted an army of addicted readers . . . the books are fast, have plenty of action and just the right degree of sex . . . Nick Carter is the American James Bond, suave, sophisticated, a killer with both the ladies and the enemy."
–The New York Times

FROM THE NICK CARTER
KILLMASTER SERIES

NICK CARTER

KILLMASTER

The Mayan Connection

CHARTER BOOKS, NEW YORK

''Nick Carter'' is a registered trademark of The Condé Nast Publications, Inc., registered in the United States Patent Office.

THE MAYAN CONNECTION

A Charter Book/published by arrangement with
The Condé Nast Publications, Inc.

PRINTING HISTORY
Charter Original/November 1984

All rights reserved.
Copyright © 1984 by The Condé Nast Publications, Inc.
This book may not be reproduced in whole
or in part, by mimeograph or any other means,
without permission. For information address:
The Berkley Publishing Group, 200 Madison Avenue,
New York, New York 10016.

ISBN: 0-441-52276-9

Charter Books are published by The Berkley Publishing Group,
200 Madison Avenue, New York, N.Y. 10016.
PRINTED IN THE UNITED STATES OF AMERICA

*Dedicated to the men of the
Secret Services of the United
States of America*

PROLOGUE

In Albany, New York, businessman Duane Michaels stood on the airport's tarmac and rubbed the cashier's check between his fingers.

"It is all there," Tiger Santos said cooly.

Michaels nodded. He was a stout man in his early forties, dressed in an expensive three-piece suit. His shoes were shined to a high gloss. He wore a diamond set in gold on his pinky finger. He reeked of money, and a love of it.

"Indeed it is," Michaels said, allowing himself a smile of success as he again read the amount on the check.

Santos returned his wallet to the hip pocket of his black satin jumpsuit. He wore black leather boots to the knees and moved with short, violent jerks.

"I'll be going now," the young Latin American said. "Montreal."

Michaels nodded again, uninterested, as Santos swung away toward the Gulfstream Jetprop 1000 that he'd just bought. It glistened like new in the afternoon sun. Airport sounds floated across the tarmac. A pickup loaded with engine parts drove past. The smells of grease and hot asphalt filled the air.

Michaels turned on his heel and walked toward his Mercedes. He snapped the check with his finger and grinned widely.

ONE

San Antonio is a colorful city even at night. Neon lights flash in brilliant oranges, yellows, and blues in the honky-tonk sections. Cowboys stagger up the sidewalks, their legs bent as if still riding horses. Pimps beat their whores. Dogs and drunks urinate on buildings. And Tex-Mex music blares from bars, too big a sound to be contained in any room, not even an outsize Texas room.

Nick Carter, Killmaster N3 of the United States' most secret agency, AXE, considered this as he shambled along the sidewalk, a bottle of Tokay clasped protectively against his side.

The street teemed with cars and people. Big old Cadillacs pulled horse trailers and waited at traffic lights next to Volkswagen bugs with fake Rolls-Royce hoods. Dodge and Chevrolet vans moved smoothly, obeying all laws as hookers in front drove and others in back accommodated johns. In San Antonio nothing is unexpected. Everything is possible.

Carter, dressed in filthy Levi's and vest, a battered Stetson pulled low over his eyes, hugged the bottle of cheap wine and meandered after his quarry. Just another faceless cowboy disappointed in the land of possibilities.

Ahead of him, the agent he trailed walked tiredly among the pedestrians, slapped off the hands of clumsy pickpockets, and shook his head at the hawkers outside bars who offered him sights he'd never seen. He too wore a cowboy disguise, but he had given up any pretense of believing in it. He'd been successful—he'd made his contact and picked up his information—and now Carter was waiting only for a moment of privacy to relieve him of his success.

Then a fist swung out from a black hole that was a doorway.

Carter ducked, then slammed an elbow into the void.

The bottle of Tokay smashed to the sidewalk as Carter felt the satisfying crunch of ribs meeting stomach and heard the screams of pain from the dark doorway.

Carter crouched low, swiveled on his heels, and watched. The quarry he'd been tailing darted into a bar with purple windows and a flashing gold neon boot outside.

The corner was suddenly quiet, wary. Drivers in cars waited at the traffic light with averted eyes. Pedestrians disappeared down the sidewalk. There were no sounds but idling engines, soft moans from the unconscious attacker in the doorway, and the distant *thud-slap* of playing cards on a felt table.

Carter cocked his head. His trained senses were as finely tuned as IBM microchips and as sensitive as exposed nerve endings. He knew he still wasn't safe.

Then he heard it.

Leather slapping brick.

Three figures leaped like uncaged animals from the brick ledge above Carter.

One dropped toward his back.

Two more fell on either side of him, trying to cut off escape.

Faster than a thought, Carter rolled and sprang untouched to his feet, Hugo, his razor-sharp stiletto, steady in his hand.

He sliced through the stocking mask of the first attacker.

Blood spurted from the man's forehead, nose, and cheek.

Carter spun as the man yelled and clutched his face. Blood poured between the man's fingers onto the sidewalk. He collapsed in a heap.

Carter kicked a revolver from the second attacker's hand, wheeled, and ripped a revolver from the third man.

The two uninjured men backed off, surprised eyes framed by the narrow slits in their stocking masks.

Carter pursued, one step at a time.

Across the sidewalk.

Past a straggly magnolia.

Over an iron grate.

And a whip lashed out, catching on the grate.

Carter tripped and fell, Hugo sliding away.

The whip released.

Carter grabbed, too late.

It returned to the attacker who'd sent it and immediately lashed out again.

Across Carter's chest.

Drawing blood and pain.

Again Carter grabbed and missed, his head spinning.

The attackers laughed.

"The great Killmaster!" the one with the whip hooted. He had a Spanish accent.

"He is not so good, eh?" the other said. "Never as good as us!" He stood to the side, arms crossed over a thin chest, his masked face thrown back, laughing. "Gringos!" He had a high, throaty voice, intense with hatred.

Carter glanced along the sidewalk and saw the attackers' revolvers far behind him. But Hugo lay close, gleaming green with light reflected from a café sign.

The whip again sang through the air.

Carter rolled, his head clearing.

The whip struck only concrete.

Carter sprang to his feet with Hugo, and in one smooth movement he sliced the whip, threw the stiletto into the whip-wielding attacker's heart, and knocked the other attacker unconscious.

The attacker with the whip now held a useless weapon, and he stood frozen in horror and surprise. Then suddenly he yanked Hugo from his heart. A brilliant red geyser gushed into the neon night, and he pitched over.

Carter picked up Hugo, cleaned him on the dead man's sweatshirt, and slipped him back into the spring-activated chamois sheath strapped to Carter's forearm from where, with the tensing of a muscle, he'd be returned to Carter's hand for action.

Carter observed the deserted sidewalk and busy street. Safe for the moment, he bent over the bloody body.

The pockets were empty, No jewelry except a cheap wristwatch with a wide band. No tags within the clothes. He pulled off the stocking mask and saw a broad, brown face with black eyebrows. Latin-American, but from which country?

Carter sensed movement beside him. The attacker he'd knocked out was on his feet, stumbling then running like a nervous woman down the sidewalk. He favored his left side.

Carter was tempted to follow, but instead his attention was caught by the edge of something white on the body below. He pulled a scrap of paper from under the wristband of the dead man's watch. A tiny piece of paper with one word printed carefully in pencil: ITZAMNA.

TWO

The café with the flashing gold neon boot was called Red Sam's. The door was open, and cigarette smoke made the night air acrid and gray even before Carter stepped inside. The long walnut bar was three-deep with thirsty oil roustabouts and cowboys. A Mexican combo played rough songs of faithless love and back-country violence.

Carter sat at a small wooden table against the wall. The table was carved with the indifferent marks of the lazy: no traditional hearts, initials, or women's breasts, but simply lines and hacked-out holes that showed someone with a sharp knife, too much time, and no imagination had sat there.

Carter leaned back so his chair rested against the wall. He lit a Marlboro—he didn't think one of his custom-made cigarettes with his initials embossed in gold on the filter went with his outfit—and stared around the room. No one bothered to look back, except for a girl with stringy hair and a beautiful face. She stared from the bar at Carter's bloody, whiplashed chest. He smiled at her and nodded. She looked at him boldly, then dropped her gaze as if to reconsider.

Carter continued to peruse the room. He'd expected his quarry to be gone, and he was right. There were plenty of cowboys, but none looked as if he would be more comfortable in a three-piece polyester suit. There were plenty of Mexicans but none had the air of a bureaucrat gone wrong.

The agent—Carter's quarry—had ducked in here and disappeared.

A waiter approached Carter's table.

"What d'yall want?" The waiter spoke to the empty space above Carter's head. He had the air of a man lost to life, so lost that his eyes couldn't meet another's for fear of being called back.

"Did you see a man about five-foot-ten in a red plaid shirt and jeans come in here about half an hour ago?" Carter asked. "Had a scar across his forehead like this." He traced a jagged line above his eyebrows and down his left temple.

"Haven't seen no one like that all day," the waiter drawled. "What d'yall want to drink?"

Carter nodded. The waiter hadn't noticed, would never notice, and if he had or could, wouldn't tell.

"Beck's," Carter said, "and give the lady another of whatever she's drinking."

The waiter followed Carter's gaze to the beautiful young woman with the long stringy hair at the bar. Embarrassed, he left to fill the order.

The sound in the street started like a distant drumming. Quickly it grew louder. The waiter put a full glass in front of the girl, then ran around the bar with five more waiters and bartenders toward the front door. Customers peeled out of the way, watching with interest. The girl looked at the drink and then at Carter. She crossed her legs and her skirt rode up over her knee.

"Out!" the bartenders yelled.

They flapped their white aprons and bellowed.

"Out! Out! Get outta here!"

The noise was like thunder, and the waiters and bartenders backed into the room.

"Yippee!" a hoarse voice shouted.

A lariat swung through the door and fell around one of the retreating bartenders. He yanked at it angrily, but it tightened and dragged him back toward the door.

The horse and rider pranced into the barroom, the cowboy

low over the speckled Appaloosa, the bartender nose to nose with the horse.

"That's MacDuff," the beautiful girl said and sat at the table with Carter. "He gets bad drunk every month or so."

The cowboy wrapped the end of the lariat around his saddlehorn, slid off the mare, and strutted up to the bar. The Appaloosa snorted, whinnied, and rolled her eyes. A customer slapped the cowboy's shoulder and handed him a drink while two waiters rushed to untie the writhing bartender.

"Of course, with his reputation," the girl continued, "MacDuff can't get away with the wildness he used to."

The Appaloosa's ears were laid back against her rust-and-white head. Her tail twitched nervously as the waiters walked her around and out the door. The bartender who'd been lassoed sank onto a chair and mopped his face. The customers reassembled at the bar around MacDuff, laughing, retelling tonight's story and others as they once again took up the serious task of drinking.

"You should be caring for that front of yours."

The girl glared at Carter's chest as if it were an insult. She had flecks of back in her blue eyes, and her cheekbones were high and good, but her honey-colored hair was in need of a good washing. She patted the matted strands back over her ears as if she knew but didn't care. She was a hooker who didn't have too high an opinion of herself.

"I appreciate your concern," Carter said seriously, "but I'm looking for someone. Soon's I find him, I'll take care of my chest."

"Who?"

She had a forthrightness that Carter liked. Direct. No games. He offered her a cigarette. She cupped his hand and stared into his eyes as he lit it. He stared back. Her eyes had the color and hidden intensity of uncut lapis lazuli.

He described his quarry. He wasn't surprised when she nodded knowingly.

"He's staying at the Saguaro Motor Inn down the street," she said. "Alone."

Part of her work was to watch everyone who came into the bar.

"How long?"

She shrugged narrow shoulders beneath a blouse with frayed collar and cuffs.

"A few days," she said.

"Thanks." Carter laid ten dollars on the table and stood up.

"You'll never find the place," she said.

She watched him, her sculpted face pinched, waiting for him to refuse her company. She was very beautiful despite her unkempt hair and shabby clothes.

"Want to show me?"

"I wouldn't mind," she replied softly.

He followed her to the door, watching her long legs prance beneath the short denim skirt. They walked out into the gaudy night. Down the street, the sidewalk was cordoned off. Three patrol cars with flashing red lights blocked a lane of traffic. The bodies had been taken away, and detectives and patrolmen were investigating. Nothing would come of it. The attackers were from some distant country that kept poor records and had little interest in dead agents.

MacDuff's mare nickered at them. The girl stroked the horse's nose, scratched behind its ears, and rubbed between the eyes. The mare was tethered to the handle of a large blue mailbox.

"See?" the girl asked Carter. "This is where she likes it."

She worked on the spot between the eyes, and the horse again nickered and blew.

"MacDuff's got a good horse," Carter said.

The girl nodded.

"Don't he know it, too. When he's sober."

They walked up the sidewalk, away from the horse and police.

"I knew you were friendly," the girl said. "I could tell."

"You were the friendly one. You were worried about my cuts."

As she walked, she swung her shoulder bag. She smelled

faintly of a nice perfume; Carter guessed she took advantage of the sample bottles on drugstore cosmetic counters.

"Business good?" Carter asked.

"Not very."

"You don't like the work."

After two blocks, the buildings got smaller with occasional untended lots in between. Weeds sprouted in sidewalk cracks and in rain gutters. Carter and the girl passed a junkyard with the remains of an old International Harvester reaper abandoned next to a locked double gate of chicken and barbed wire.

"See it?" the girl asked and pointed.

On the far side of the junkyard, away from the street on a gravel road, were a cluster of ramshackle cottages that had once been white. They shone like old bones in the moonlight. Before them was a painted sign illuminated by an overhead light: Saguaro Motor Inn—Air Conditioning—Refrigerators. The light was so small that the sign was almost lost in the night.

"I think you can help me," Carter said speculatively.

"I don't have to."

"I'll pay."

She flipped gravel with the toe of her sandal. He looked at the quiet street. Only an old pickup was parked at a curb three doors away. In the faint glow of a streetlight, Carter saw the silhouettes of two figures, heads together—lovers—sitting in the front seat.

"What's your name?" Carter asked the girl.

"I'm nineteen. I left home when I was twelve."

"Do you want to help?" he asked.

"Linda," she said. "My name's Linda."

He held her chin and looked into her lapis lazuli eyes. She trembled and watched him intently. His chest and head hurt. He bent and kissed her. Her mouth was sweet, clean. Her breasts firm and hot. She leaned into him, shuddering with pleasure, and he pulled her closer.

"What do you want me to do?" she asked.

THREE

The night sky was thick with twinkling stars, cleared of smog by a rising wind off the San Antonio River. Katydids and crickets sang. The grass was sun-dried and fragrant. In the next block someone pumped an accordian song of fast adventure.

Nick Carter stood at the corner of his quarry's ramshackle motel cottage and considered the darkness. Sounds and smells vary from country to country, but the mystique of night remains.

Linda walked up the gravel driveway to the cottage door. The cottage's single front window was blank, the shade drawn over the dull flicker of a television within. Carter listened to the girl's footsteps crunch against the gravel, the blur of television voices, and the warm wind rustle nearby sage and scrub trees. The sounds were heightened by the potential for violence that darkness brings.

The girl knocked.

"Yes?" a man's voice said.

The door opened a crack. Carter slid along the wall toward the door at an angle the quarry could not see. Light and the sweet smell of rum spilled from the door's crack. The quarry had been watching a Spanish-language TV station.

"I'm your present," the girl purred.

She slouched against the doorjamb. Her skirt lifted above

13

the shapely legs. Her breathing intensified, breasts rising against the thin cloth of her blouse.

"Happy Birthday," she said.

Carter could feel the quarry's stare.

"From MacDuff and the boys at the bar," she said.

Her eyes were heavy-lidded. Her pelvis tilted, her breathing deep and irregular. She gave off a scent of lust thick enough to bottle, and the quarry leaned forward hungrily.

"MacDuff?" he said eagerly.

She nodded and stared up through lashes thick with mascara.

"But it is not my birthday," he said.

The girl slowly ran a finger down the quarry's cheek and chest, stopping at his belt buckle. He sighed deeply.

"It doesn't have to be," she cooed.

He let her push him back into the motel room, grinning from ear to ear with anticipation.

Until he saw Nick Carter.

Carter kicked the door closed, Hugo in hand.

The quarry was a dark man with small, pretty features in a broad face. He was in his fifties, a look of permanent disappointment engraved on his face in a deeply etched pattern of downturned lines. He flung the girl into the television set.

The girl and set crashed to the floor. The set sparked, and she cried out, holding her side. Carter half turned to her.

"I'm all right!" she shouted.

It was only a half turn, only a moment, but it was long enough for an old guerrilla fighter. The quarry jumped from behind and wrapped an arm around Carter's throat.

Carter jabbed an elbow back.

A piston into the quarry's stomach.

The stomach had been behind a desk too long; it was soft and pulpy.

The quarry gasped and weakened.

Carter broke free, whirling around.

"Where is it?" Carter demanded, pointing Hugo at the retreating man.

"Nada!" the quarry panted and threw a plastic chair. "I tell you nothing!"

Carter ducked.

The quarry ran to the dresser and pulled out a revolver.

Carter hurled Hugo through the air and pinned the quarry's red plaid sleeve to the cracked plaster wall. The revolver dangled, useless.

The girl laughed.

"I saw you get it," Carter said, walking slowly toward the man.

The quarry growled and pulled frantically at the stiletto.

"It would be easier on you to tell me where it is," Carter said, now close.

The stiletto popped from the wall.

The quarry crouched free, red-eyed with rum and rage, Hugo in one hand and the revolver in the other.

Carter shook his head.

"Damned fool," he muttered.

Before the quarry could aim, Carter kicked Hugo into the bathroom and rammed the side of his rock-hard hand into the quarry's ribs.

Ribs cracked and broke, and the man doubled over.

The revolver fell.

Carter scooped up the gun and pointed it at the quarry's head.

"This isn't the way to get a promotion," Carter said.

The girl giggled again.

The quarry lunged, a bull elephant gone mad, pushing his head into Carter's belly.

He shoved Carter back across the room. The gun dropped from Carter's hand under the furious force of the quarry.

"No!" the girl screamed.

The pair crashed through the window shade and window.

Glass shattered, slivers flying through the air, exploding into the night.

Carter hit the ground outside with the other agent on top, but a second later the quarry scrambled up and ran away across the gravel.

Carter raced after the man who now held his sides as if in a straightjacket of pain.

Carter hurled himself forward and tackled the escaping agent in the sickly light of the motel sign.

Gravel flew and crunched as the girl ran up to them.

The old guerrilla fighter twisted, trying to bring his knee up between Carter's legs. His face was fierce with determination.

One shot rang out.

Sharp and startling.

The quarry fell into the weeds beside the motel. Blood poured from his neck into the dry ground. He jerked and lay still.

The girl stood somber, the agent's revolver limp at her side. She looked up at Carter with round, stricken eyes.

"He would've killed you," Linda said.

"Ten years ago he might've hurt me. But not now," Carter said. He gazed sadly at the crumpled man whose life emptied into a foreign land. "He was tired of a dead-end desk job. He wanted excitement, adventure again. Something to believe in."

"Who was he?"

"A Cuban agent."

Carter knelt and searched through the agent's clothing.

"How do you know?" she asked.

Carter worked rapidly, dumping wallet, credit cards, handkerchief, everything into a pile under the dim light.

"We're all players in the same game," he answered. "We know one another, if only by reputation."

What Carter was looking for was not in the man's belongings. He took off the agent's shirt and examined it. He unbuckled the belt.

"What are you doing?" Linda asked, her voice rising.

"I know you're afraid," Carter said, still searching. He took off the agent's pants. "Go if you like."

The girl twisted her head, looking around, obviously frightened. Cars passed infrequently in the street. The dark pickup was still the only vehicle parked at the curb. The jukebox music and drunken laughter were distant, safe sounds. The complex of dilapidated cottages was quiet and had the feeling of being deserted even though lights glowed in some cottages. In this part of town, only the reckless or foolish investigated gunfire.

"Who are you?" Linda whispered.

"Your employee."

Carter stared at the naked man, vulnerable and flaccid in death. He knew the information wouldn't be in the room; the agent would keep it on him.

Carter picked up the penis and searched around the testicles. Nothing. Then he ran his fingers down the almost hairless legs.

"You must be a spy," the girl decided.

"Must be," Carter echoed.

He found the tiny black dot between the first and second toes of the left foot. He took an addressed envelope from his pocket, stuck the dot in the upper-right corner, licked a stamp, and put it over the microdot.

"Wow!" the girl exclaimed. "You really *are* a spy!"

Carter grinned at her. She was a street urchin again, dirty-faced but now sparkling with youth and vitality.

"We'd better get out of here," Carter said.

He took her hand, and they walked away from the naked dead man laid out like a slab of meat beneath the dim sign of the Saguaro Motor Inn. They headed back toward San Antonio's honky-tonk sounds of sobbing guitars and blaring trumpets.

FOUR

To the north, hidden by the night, were the hills that Spanish friars had chosen as a backdrop when they had founded San Antonio in 1718. Tonight, as usual, music and the hot, oily aromas of chili and tacos wafted across the old city called affectionately by residents San Antone. Others didn't love San Antone—or Texas. After visiting there in 1866, General Philip H. Sheridan observed, "If I owned Texas and all hell, I would rent out Texas and live in hell."

Nick Carter reflected on this as he heard the lone pickup's motor turn on. Some might hate Texas, but others loved it enough to make the state one of the fastest growing in the nation and San Antone the tenth largest metropolis. But along with progress came evil. And evil was attracted to growth and wealth to feed on—and to poverty to hide behind.

The old pickup's motor idled and the headlights came on, catching Carter and Linda as if spotlighted on a stage. She turned to stare. The battered pickup moved slowly up the street, following them. Carter hurried Linda along the sidewalk.

As the bar with the flashing gold neon boot came into view, they heard the pickup's tires squeal with a sudden burst of speed.

MacDuff's Appaloosa mare tossed her head and whinnied. She was still tethered to the mailbox.

19

"What is it?" Linda's face was stretched in fright.

Carter yanked the girl into a run.

"I don't know," he said tersely. "It should be over."

They raced down the sidewalk.

At this late hour, traffic was light. A few sports cars and Lincolns.

The pickup roared behind them, rapidly catching up.

Using his body as a shield, Carter slid the envelope into the mail slot. The girl leaned against the box, panting. The horse nuzzled her shoulder.

Shots from the pickup rang out in the neon night, spitting into the concrete around them. Heads, shoulders, and hands waving drinks emerged from the bar with the flashing gold boot.

Carter leaped onto the mare, pulled the girl up behind him, and turned the horse up the street.

"MacDuff!" someone called into the bar.

Carter and Linda galloped away, gunfire streaking alongside them, away from the mailbox that contained crucial information for David Hawk, head of AXE and protector of security secrets the President of the United States could entrust to no other.

"They're catching up to us!" the girl screamed.

The horse's hooves reverberated against the street like a drum roll.

Carter aimed the horse around a parked low-slung Porsche, then down a dark narrow alleyway between two bars, too narrow for the pickup to follow them. Red, white, and green lanterns—the colors of Mexico—glowed festively in the distance at the end of the long alley.

Suddenly, headlights burst down the alleyway, illuminating the horse and its riders.

Doors opened and slammed shut.

The mare pounded on toward the sounds of a mariachi band.

Shots bit into the buildings on either side.

Running footsteps pursued them.

Carter and Linda hunched low over the horse, and rode into the patio party, where they were slowed by the throng.

An ornate water fountain splashed, entertainers in swirling costumes danced, champagne corks popped, and—on the far side of the patio—an open sliding glass door led into a home or business from which some partygoers watched in amusement.

"Compadre!" a man yelled at Carter, raising his glass in salute.

"Is this part of the entertainment?" one woman wanted to know.

"If it isn't, it should be," said her companion.

A white-coated waiter lifted a tray of full champagne goblets for Carter and Linda as they walked the mare by.

"Dom Perignon!" the waiter announced.

Carter and the girl each bent for glasses.

"Gracias," Carter said politely.

"Thanks," said the girl in her soft Texas accent.

The celebrators cheered and patted the sweating Appaloosa as Carter and Linda rode around the tinkling fountain and into the plushly carpeted living room of some wealthy San Antone citizen.

"Isn't that MacDuff's mare?" someone asked.

"Sure does look like her," agreed another.

The mare held her head high as she stepped past mosaic coffee tables displaying objets d'art. She shied away from the fireplace hearth spilling with red roses and snorted at a six-foot specimen of Spanish armor guarding the entrance to the parqueted foyer.

Behind them, Carter saw four men weaving through the crowd. All four looked Mexican; all had Indian features. One of them wore a shiny black jumpsuit, while the three others were dressed in green military fatigues with no identification patches. Two of them had been in the cab of the pickup pretending to be lovers, and the other two must have been lying in the truck bed out of sight.

The party guests stared at the out-of-place intruders, and

the intruders stared at Carter.

"*Salud!*" Carter said, raising his glass to the room of Texans.

"*Salud! Salud! Salud!*" shouted the partygoers.

They drank the champagne. *Brut*—beautifully dry.

Carter leaned down, set his and Linda's goblets on a high sideboard, and swung open the eight-foot-high walnut front doors.

Gunfire exploded into the helmet of the suit of armor.

Pieces of metal scarred the immaculate plaster ceiling and walls.

The Texans ducked.

And came up mad.

Enormous roars of indignation swelled the room.

Two big Texans instantly coldcocked two of the pursuers, who collapsed uncomplaining onto the thick carpet, one with a Luger in his hand.

A woman in emeralds, silk, and high-heeled shoes stomped the foot of the third man from the pickup. Her companion punched the man's stomach and then his jaw. The injured man grabbed the elegant woman for support, but she kneed him and shoved him to the floor.

The fourth intruder—the one wearing the black jumpsuit—stood jittery, trying to decide what to do in the room where he was so badly outnumbered. He had a young, cruel face, and kept his hand inside the deep V of material on his chest where Carter knew he kept a gun. But the crowd didn't notice. They swarmed toward the man, laughing and talking, putting more and more people between him and Carter and the girl.

"Let's get out of here," Carter said.

"They liked the way you set the glasses down so politely," Linda said as they again walked the Appaloosa to the front doors.

"The Texas frontier spirit of generosity and instant retribution," Carter said.

She looked at him and smiled.

"You knew they'd like the mare, too."

Carter grinned as they stepped through the foyer, but there was a cool glint in his eyes as he looked back at his pursuers, who were picking themselves up and retreating.

"Now I've got to find a telephone," he said.

He clicked softly to the mare, and she walked daintily down the mansion's brick steps, across the sidewalk, and into the quiet street.

Carter and Linda rode MacDuff's speckled horse along El Paseo del Rio, skirting the glassy jade flow of the San Antonio River. They passed a sign giving directions to the Alamo, "the cradle of Texas liberty." It was now a carefully restored mission, a stone emblem to the tragedy of man's folly and greed. Davy Crockett and Jim Bowie died in that battle in 1836, and only seven Americans out of almost two hundred survived the Alamo slaughter, but they were captured and ordered killed by Mexican General Santa Anna. "Though tortured before they were killed, these unfortunates died without complaining and humiliating themselves," Carter remembered one of Santa Anna's staff members had written.

"What are you thinking about?" Linda asked.

"Liberty. Its price," Carter said. He looked ahead. "There's that telephone booth I need."

Carter put in his dime and dialed.

"What's wrong?" Hawk's gruff voice was suspicious. He'd not expected Carter to call in, escpecially in the middle of the night.

Carter kept his back to Linda and the horse. No need for her to know more than she had to.

"You should receive the information within a couple of days," Carter said. "It's in the package we agreed upon. Mailed tonight."

If Hawk were the kind of man who sighed with relief, Carter knew he would sigh now. Instead, Hawk would lean back in bed, reach to the brass cigar box on his bedside table, and carefully select a cigar. He would roll it, bite the end off, and light it.

Carter heard the click of a butane lighter and smiled.

"I trust you know what time it is," Hawk growled.

"Yes, sir. Four A.M. in Washington. I have something new to report."

"It will be dawn here shortly, N3. It is discouraging to try to fall asleep once it is dawn."

"Three guys jumped me before I got to the Cuban. One of them had a scrap of paper on him. Only one word. Itzamná. The Mayan god. Thought the connection might be important. Also, four men in an old pickup tried to get me after I got the agent. I think they were watching *him*, not me. No idea who they could be."

Carter heard Hawk inhale and blow. By now there would be a cloud of noxious smoke above Hawk's bed.

"Any other identification on the three who jumped you?" Hawk asked.

"Nothing."

"And you're sure the ones in the pickup weren't Cubans? They weren't after you?"

"I'm sure."

He heard Hawk puff again.

"Fascinating," Hawk murmured.

"The microdot should clear up the Cuban mystery down there," Carter said.

Far off, Hawk cleared his throat, his mind made up.

"You have a new assignment, Nick. The FBI, State, the FAA, and the Justice Department have all called in the last twenty-four hours. We've got an irate taxpayer in Albany whose jet has been stolen. He's got money and inherited influence—just enough to irritate people with work to do," Hawk said and chomped the cigar. "But his greed may have been helpful. The taxpayer thought he'd sold his jet, but the cashier's check was phony. The buyer has vanished. And the jet's been found abandoned in New Mexico with no clues except a torn map of southern Mexico with Itzamná scrawled on it."

"Texas, Albany, and now New Mexico."

"Precisely," Hawk said. "The taxpayer has been complaining to every agency he can think of. He wants his money back. But it doesn't end there."

"Barkov?" Carter said, the hair on the back of his neck rising. Colonel Maxim Barkov—not his real name, of course—was the KGB chief in Mexico. An irrational killer. Very useful to the KGB.

"You remember the report," Hawk said approvingly. "You confirm my ability to choose the best personnel." Hawk cleared his throat after the unaccustomed compliment. "British MI5 has passed on the most recent decoding. I've been wondering whether to act or wait. You've settled the issue. Here's the situation. The KGB is worried about Barkov. Odd actions and strange reports from him to them. From what MI5's been able to intercept, the KGB may be on the verge of either pulling Barkov or investigating him. That in itself isn't particularly significant—Russian spies do come and go—but one report on Barkov mentioned Itzamná. It's puzzling the KGB, too."

"Do you want me to start in Albany or Mexico City?"

Hawk gave a short, pleased laugh.

"Albany," he said. "Go see the taxpayer—Duane Michaels is his name. Then find that pilot. He's the most direct link we've got to whoever or whatever Itzamná is."

As Hawk gave Carter the details of how to locate Michaels, Carter heard the oncoming sounds of running feet, whoops of success, and the mare's high-pitched whinny.

"Nick!" Linda shouted.

Carter whirled around.

The street was full of cowboys running toward Carter, Linda, and the mare. MacDuff was leading, waving his Stetson in a big circle above his head, his handsome face flushed and grinning from ear to ear.

MacDuff pointed an accusatory finger at Carter, but his eyes glowed with merriment.

"Horse thief!" he shouted and leaped up behind Linda. She struggled to get off, but MacDuff laughed and wrapped an arm around her. He leaned down for the reins, flicked his heels against the mare's sides, and wheeled her off down the street.

"I'll buy Linda a drink!" MacDuff shouted back to Carter. "Best ride she'll ever have!"

Carter nodded and waved, his mind now on the best jet connections to Albany.

Linda settled back against MacDuff, resigned, and he hugged her.

The crowd of drunk cowboys surged and reorganized themselves to follow the Appaloosa, cowboy, and girl back up El Paseo del Rio toward their favorite honky-tonk bar.

FIVE

Albany, capital of the State of New York, displayed its Dutch heritage in colonial architecture, tulip festivals, and prominent names such as Schuyler, Van Rensselaer, and Erastus Corning. Where San Antonio had the excitement and dazzle of frontier fighters, Albany had the hushed dignity of successful bankers, businessmen, educators, and politicians.

Nick Carter thought about this as he rode up the walnut-paneled elevator to the top floor of the granite and limestone office building. Female office workers in tasteful dresses and pumps, businessmen in tailored three-piece suits, and an unnecessary elevator operator in short navy jacket and pillbox hat didn't necessarily mean money. But secretaries in other cities sometimes wore polyester slacks with elastic waists. Businessmen tried to fool their peers and clients with off-the-rack suits from Penney's. And elevators with pushbuttons didn't need operators to inquire respectfully, "Which floor, sir?"

Carter nodded at the sharp-eyed elevator operator and stepped off at the top floor. He walked to a wall of plate glass windows that looked across the old Dutch city and the Hudson River. San Antonio's money was ostentatious. Albany's was tasteful—hidden but just as powerful. The real excitement in this city was behind closed doors.

Carter smoothed the lapels of his Savile Row suit, adjusted

the sapphire ring on his right hand, and noted with approval the shine on his wing tips. As he walked toward the secretary who would be Michaels's, he took out his gold cigarette case.

"Duane Michaels," he told her.

"Your name and business?"

She was a straight-from-the-bottle redhead with a long, aquiline nose, pinched mouth, and too much powder. The powder hid freckles that on another woman would be flaunted and sexy. He watched as she calculated by his clothes how much he was worth.

"Name's Nelson Calhoun," he announced.

He opened the case, took out a monogrammed cigarette, and slipped the case back inside his jacket.

Her eyes flickered. Gold, the eyes said, five hundred dollars.

"My business is working for H. Banning Michaels," Carter said, lighting the cigarette. "Mr. Michaels wants me to see his son about a missing aircraft."

"Of course, sir."

Being impressed held more value to her than thinking did. She pushed the intercom switch.

"Mr. Nelson Calhoun to see you regarding the Gulfstream," she said.

"Who's he?" said a disembodied, irritated voice. "Not the newspapers!"

"From your father," she said archly, glancing at Carter conspiratorially.

There was silence from the other end of the intercom.

"You might tell him that his father has a solution to the problem," Carter said mildly.

"Mr. Calhoun says—" she began.

"I heard him! Send him in!"

Carter walked through double oak doors with brass hardware that looked as if it came from an old whaling ship. Michaels sat behind a long, wide, highly polished desk. The desk was neatly piled with stacks of papers. A Cross ballpoint pen lay open, ready to use. Whatever kind of businessman Michaels was, at least he was one who worked.

Michaels looked Carter up and down, stood, and extended a hand.

"What does the old man say?" Michaels asked.

Carter shook the hand and and sat in a red leather chair. Michaels liked to get to the point. He had a fleshy face, a paunch, and a sense about him of unimaginative competence.

"Do you want the jet repaired?" Carter asked.

"Hell, no! It's a white elephant. Outlived its usefulness."

"No chance of insurance money?"

"Only to repair it." Michaels leaned forward, his flabby chest spreading across the papers. "I don't want it repaired. I don't want to waste time selling it again. I want my *money*."

"The buyer pay you a fair price?"

Michaels's face flushed.

"I pay taxes," Michaels complained. "I pay a lot of taxes! I expect to be protected, not defrauded!"

"I see."

Carter smoked. As he'd expected, Michaels had overcharged for the jet, and his greed had made him careless.

"Your father is prepared to make up your loss in exchange for information," Carter said.

Michaels brightened. His fingers ran like crabs across the desk top.

"The *entire* loss?" Michaels asked.

"What the jet's really worth."

"It's worth top dollar."

"It *was* worth comparatively little," Carter corrected. "It was old. Overused and not maintained. You had it washed and polished, and sold it for new. Now it's an abandoned wreck in a New Mexico desert. The longer you wait, the less chance you have of getting anything at all for it."

Michaels pressed his fingers together into a church steeple. He rested his chin on the tops of his fingers.

"Why does he want information?" Michaels asked cagily.

Michaels was searching for something to barter with. He couldn't help himself. A deal was much better if the other guy got screwed.

"We're talking about H. Banning Michaels," Carter said

and smiled. "He doesn't have to tell you a damned thing. His money talks."

Michaels the son stood and walked to the windows. He looked out. Clouds like mounds of whipped cream had formed across the horizon. Michaels glanced at the clouds, then looked down on the city. He knew he wasn't going to get a better deal. His father was a good businessman.

"What does he want to know?" Michaels said at last, his back still to Carter. His father had four times the wealth Michaels had, and control of a trust fund Michaels wouldn't get until the old man died.

"Everything you remember about the buyer and where he might be headed."

"All right," Michaels said briskly, staring down at the city. He wanted the interview ended and Carter out of sight. "He said his name was Tiger Santos. Ridiculous name, but it was on the cashier's check. He was dressed outrageously. Wore a black jumpsuit made out of some kind of shiny material . . ."

Carter's eyes narrowed.

"And black boots?" he said. "Almost like a storm trooper's?"

"Yes, yes," Michaels said, waving a hand indifferently. "What else would you expect?"

"And his nationality?"

"Mexican . . . Spanish . . . how would I know?" Michaels replied, annoyed. "I told you his name was Santos."

Carter nodded and thought about the four men from the pickup the night before, remembered the one with the cruel face and shiny black jumpsuit. Carter lit another cigarette.

"Go on," he told Michaels.

"Well, I figured the check was good because he looked like one of those hyped-up drugrunners you read about." Michaels barked a short, bitter laugh. "Joke was on me. When the check bounced, I tried to track him down through my contacts. He'd filed a flight plan to Montreal at the

Albany airport, but there's no record of his arrival in Montreal. Then I went to the authorities. That's all I know.''

"Were the jet's tanks full?"

"Don't know." Michaels shrugged. He didn't care either.

Carter put out his cigarette and watched the square, overweight back in the expensive suit. Michaels loved money even more than he hated his father.

"I appreciate your help," Carter said politely and stood.

Michaels turned. The thick clouds on Albany's horizon were turning gray with potential rain.

"When do I get a check?" Michaels asked.

"Mr. Michaels will be in touch."

Carter walked to the door.

"How do I know you're really from my father?" Sudden worry sharpened Michaels's voice.

"You don't."

Carter walked through the doors, past the secretary who smiled hungrily, and toward the elevators. He heard Michaels's doors close. Michaels, who had not spoken directly to his father in five years, would have the secretary make the call.

"First floor, sir?" the elevator operator asked.

Carter nodded and stepped into the enclosure that smelled faintly of good pipe tobacco. The elevator moved silently downward.

No one but Hawk knew Carter was in Albany. AXE's need for secret information had to be protected. Duane Michaels had once again been suckered by his own greed.

Nick Carter walked behind the airport counter and flashed the wallet with the official-looking gold badge. It wasn't real, but it was close. With AXE's spectacular technology, its equipment department could duplicate just about anything in the world. But the clever AXE technical staff had discovered that ersatz was more effective than exact. Exact copies bothered people; they sensed intuitively that something was wrong, even though they couldn't tell you what it was. But give them something slightly inferior—ersatz—and, like inflation and plastic automobile bumpers, most believed it was real every time.

"Plainclothesman?" the boyish-looking airport employee whispered hopefully, looking up from the badge. It said United States of America and Government Agent, and top and bottom crescents framed a bald eagle in profile.

"Detective," Carter admitted, dropping his voice to a conspiratorial whisper. "I need the flight plan Tiger Santos filed two days ago. He bought Duane Michaels's Gulfstream Commander." Carter slid the wallet containing the badge back inside his pocket.

"I remember." The young man rubbed his hands and went to work. "Been getting a lot of action on that one. Mr. Michaels sent some people in. They went through everything. Not that I give information to just anyone. . . . Oh, yes. Here it is. Very popular flight plan. And it is good to help the law. People with important jobs need to stick together. Want a copy?"

"I'd appreciate it."

"No trouble at all."

Carter took the copy from the smiling clerk, whose face practically glowed with excitement. Clerical routine had not dulled his enjoyment of life.

"Thanks," Carter said. "You know your job."

The young man was speechless with pleasure. Carter shook his hand and left.

"That was a detective," the clerk confided to the next customer. "*Very* important man."

Carter smiled inwardly as he read the flight plan. He noted that the tanks had checked out with just enough fuel to get Santos to Montreal. He memorized the number that would be painted behind the jet's cantilevered wings. Then he looked up into the busy airport, saw telephone stalls, and sauntered casually to them. As he walked, his mind worked, putting together the few clues he had, figuring the odds.

SIX

The sky was almost gaudy with the colors of sunset. Reds, oranges, and purples spread over the horizon as the sun settled to Nick Carter's right. In the Hamilton Westwind III he'd found waiting in Albany, he flew over Kingston, and would soon be over Poughkeepsie, following—if his thinking were correct—Tiger Santos.

The Pratt & Whitney turboprop engines droned and vibrated reassuringly through the steering and into Carter's hands. He liked to fly, liked the feeling of being suspended over the earth. For a time it made him different. Set apart by borrowed wings. And the earth rotating below was distant with its global problems of avarice, disloyalty, and the perverted values Carter fought daily.

As he swung the aircraft west to avoid the traffic congestion above New York City, he thought about Linda. He wished for a moment he wasn't committed to the importance of his work. But a man had to follow his beliefs. Perhaps he would meet her again when there was time.

He angled south again, the sunset washed away by the night's grays and blacks. Lights below twinkled like stars. Highways were defined in streaks of white and red. Tiger Santos had had just enough fuel in the Gulfstream to comfortably fly north to Montreal. But he had not gone there. He hadn't wanted anyone to know his real destination. He had

33

gone south instead and ultimately abandoned the plane in New Mexico. What was the map of southern Mexico doing in the cabin? Carter wondered.

The Westwind that Hawk had sent Carter was stripped of passenger seats. Because it was lighter now, the turbojet would get great distance with its oversize tanks. The tanks carried 740 gallons, comfortably more than Santos's fuel maximum of 474 gallons. Carter wanted the flexibility of distance without refueling. And he wanted the cargo pod that Hawk had sent. The pod contained two General Electric miniguns and a special suitcase with AXE clothes and small equipment.

Considering Santos's limited fuel, his jet could just have made Philadelphia. Carter flew in a straight line toward the city and circled above Philadelphia International Airport. A thin, scudding bank of clouds was far above him. Below, the runways were marked clearly, the lights flashing in sequence with each plane that went in. To the east was the Delaware River, black as ink.

Carter listened to the chatter of air controllers.

"Identify yourself, Westwind!" one demanded of Carter. "Identify yourself!"

Carter ignored the increasingly angry voice. Instead he listened to the other controllers and watched the sky around him.

Slowly he descended until a break came in the traffic.

He tipped the turbojet's nose into a quick landing descent. The electronically controlled retractable landing gear dropped into place. He would go in secretly. If the G.E. miniguns were discovered, he'd have too much to explain.

The plane's three-blade propellers hummed, seeming to catch the air as if it had substance.

Land rushed up.

Lights that had been pinpricks were suddenly walls.

He flew the turbojet between the walls of flashing lights and skillfully touched the wheels onto the runway.

He slowed.

Around him other planes came in, their engines screaming and roaring.

He taxied the Westwind toward maintenance buildings that loomed large and gray in the night. Lights made bright rectangles of the windows where mechanics worked overtime.

Carter parked the plane in front of a building that was closed for the night. It was recessed between two larger buildings and gave the AXE plane some privacy.

He hopped out of the portside door, his Top-Siders springy against the tarmac. He wore the clothes of a man of leisure: tan silk slacks, simple plaid Madras shirt, and loden green Sol jacket that showed good taste. His appearance would generate no questions, only approval, at the Philadelphia airport. Behind in the jet were his AXE suitcase and his faithful companion, Wilhelmina, a 9mm Luger. Now he carried only Hugo and Pierre, the tiny gas bomb strapped to the inside of his upper thigh. He was after information, not bodies. And he was in the United States, not in danger. He didn't want innocent people killed. He would run on his wits, the surest weapon of all.

Carter strolled into the main terminal of Philadelphia International. Instantly he noticed the security guards. There were too many of them, and they were alert.

He watched their eyes scan passengers, stewardesses, pilots, desk personnel, cafeteria workers, soldiers on leave, young mothers with babies—everyone. They tried to mingle unobtrusively, and those out of uniform were more successful. Still, their roving eyes gave them away.

Carter took out his cigarette case and walked up to one in a shabby brown business suit. The man had heavy cheeks blue with a need to shave even though he'd probably shaved once that day already.

"Would you happen to have a light?" Carter asked and smiled.

The man looked at him once, twice, and stared suspiciously.

"Sorry," Carter said. "I think someone stole my lighter."

Carter opened the gold cigarette case, selected a cigarette, and held out the case to the security guard.

The terminal swarmed with people. Babies cried. Machines clattered. The air was thick with sound and too many stale odors.

The guard glanced around, allowed his eyes to dull with tiredness, then he chose one of Carter's cigarettes.

"Thanks," the security man said.

From his pocket he took a book of matches with the name of a local restaurant imprinted in watery blue and lit Carter's cigarette, then his own.

They puffed in companionable silence.

Carter finished first and dropped the butt into an airport ashtray.

"Must've had some excitement around here," he said conversationally.

Carter guessed the security guard had been a heavyweight boxer or football player at one time. He had the beefy shoulders, chest, and belly that came with the right kind of build augmented by carbohydrates and rigorous exercise. Now he was in his fifties, the muscles dissolving into fat, and he'd quit lying to himself that life was going to be a series of wins.

"Yeah," the guard said. "Some."

He ground out the cigarette on the floor, took a packet of Sen-Sen from his jacket, and dropped Sen-Sen granules on his tongue.

"More than the usual smuggling and dope?" Carter asked.

Already the guard smelled of licorice from the Sen-Sen. A good way to disguise the taste of a stomach gone sour with disillusionment.

"Who're you, buddy?" the guard asked.

His tired eyes completed one last scan of the enormous room and settled on Carter.

"FAA," Carter said with authority. "Investigating an airplane theft. Took place in Albany. We think the pilot might've brought it here to refuel or for some other reason."

Carter recited the missing jet's serial number and took out the wallet with the fake gold badge. It was a combination that convinced the guard. The man's eyelids lowered with emotion when Carter said the plane's number, so the look that took in the badge was only a cursory glance.

"Three people dead," the guard said curtly. "Friends of mine. One more in the hospital, intensive care."

"The pilot?"

"Joker in a black clown suit. Got away clean," the guard said bitterly. "When I was that age, I was skating with the Toronto Maple Leafs. Goalie on the team that won the Stanley in '47. We worked together. Played together. Helped each other. A real team." The guard lifted his sagging chin and made a circle of his arms to include the entire airport. "That bastard sneaks in here, kills good men, and leaves laughing. What the hell's the world coming to?"

The guard's face was masked in the thick veneer that years of dealing with the public had given him. But now, outraged misery showed through as if the mask were glass. It was a new world where old values were laughed at.

"He flying the Gulfstream?" Carter inquired.

"The same. I've seen a lot where I've been. Liars, cheaters, con artists. What does it mean?"

The guard didn't want an answer to the question. Didn't believe there was an answer. But it was good to ask anyway.

"What happened?"

"Far as I can tell, nothing," the big man said. "Landed over by the steam roller. No one particularly noticed him. Made arrangements for fueling. Paid cash. No big deal. He'd got no clearance to land, but the jet was small and the airport's busy. It happens. Same time, three of my men were searching a small cargo plane suspected of carrying cocaine. So the fuel attendant makes some remarks to a friend about the pilot's getup. Nothing loud, but they start laughing. Called him 'Fairy-pants,' I was told. So the pilot takes offense, rips his money back, and shoots the attendant dead. Runs back to his plane just as my three men barrel out of the jet. He stops long enough to kill two of them and get the other through the spine. Then he flies out, laughing like a hyena at the air controllers.''

The guard shifted from one foot to another, now tired all over.

''So you've been put on double duty,'' Carter said.

''People upstairs say we've been too lax. Shouldn't have let it happen. Not in Philadelphia.'' A short burst of pride was in his voice.

''Any leads on the pilot?''

The guard's face sank again into exhaustion, not just the exhaustion of too many hours on the job, but the frustrated exhaustion of working in a world no longer familiar.

''None,'' he said abruptly.

''Ms. Julia Cunningham. Please report to Lost and Found,'' a metallic voice said over the airport's loudspeaker system. ''Ms. Julia Cunningham.''

The guard sighed.

''That's me,'' he said and extended a hand. ''Hope you find the bastard.''

Carter watched the man's broad, wrinkled suitcoat disappear toward a white customer telephone on an airline counter. His sharp eyes quickly noted that other security guards were converging on other white elephones. Ms. Julia Cunningham was not the code name for just the man Carter had been talking with, but was a general call for all guards to report in.

Carter strode across the airport lobby, ducked around a corner, and ran down a deserted hallway. It had been five years since he'd been in the airport, but his mind had been trained to remember details. He pushed through a door marked Exit and Locked, and was hit by the sudden freshness of unfiltered, unprocessed air.

He took a deep breath, stuck his hands into the pockets of his expensive slacks, and sauntered toward the fueling area where Tiger Santos had killed three men and injured a fourth two days before.

A man with grease to his elbows, a dead cigar butt in his mouth, and critical look in his eyes glanced up at Carter.

"Who're you?" He pulled a wrench from the underbelly of a light transport. "FBI? Let's see the badge."

Carter grinned.

"You win," he said. "Guess I can't fool you."

He showed the mechanic the badge. The man squinted and grunted.

"Only the FBI can afford clothes like yours," the mechanic said, pleased with himself. "If it's about that crazy guy night before last, I wasn't here. Edie was."

The mechanic jerked his head at a young woman in coveralls sitting crosslegged beside a fuel pump, reading a thick book.

Carter walked across the tarmac. In the distance, jets taxied into the night, and airport buses and trucks made rounds, carefully stopping at runway intersections. The fueling area was bright with light, and only the faint odor of gas indicated the giant lake of gallons available there.

As Carter approached, the girl looked up, then stood, She was thin, flatchested, with curiosity permanently imprinted on her angular face.

"I understand you saw the murders," Carter said as he stopped beside her.

"I did," she admitted. "Why do you want to know?"

"CIA," Carter said. "Tracking the pilot. He was in an incident in Paris."

"That would be right," Edie said. 'The CIA does only international investigations. Do you have identification?" She watched Carter, interested but still appraising.

Carter held up the open wallet with the badge.

"Your agent's number and CIA aren't on it," she said, peering closely at it and then at him.

"That's because of the agency's need for secrecy," he said easily.

He closed the wallet. She didn't protest.

"Not even Washington, D.C., is on it," she said.

"With the CIA, it's the country. United States of America. You saw that."

"That's right," she said, brightening. "What do you want to know?"

"Were you talking with the attendant who was killed?"

"I was mopping up," Edie said, clasping the book against her chest. "Jack and Billy were laughing about the pilot."

"And you?"

She was thin but soft. Older than she looked. Probably twenty-five or twenty-six. She cradled the heavy hardcover novel in her arms and looked off across the tarmac as if it were the sea. In an earlier generation she would have affected glasses to warn people she had a brain that liked to consider life.

"Watching," she said. "I didn't think the boys were funny, but no one's asked me that. All the police wanted to know was whether the pilot shot Billy and the others like Jack said."

"But you saw something else."

She brought her gaze back to Carter.

"How did you know?" she asked, her eyes big and round.

Carter shrugged and smiled.

"I'm not really surprised," she decided. "You would know. You're different, too." She watched him as she talked. "Two men. I wouldn't have noticed anything except they were dressed too dark and they moved too fast. They had black sweaters and pants on, and they ran to the jet without looking around—like they'd done their looking before they ran. You know what I mean?"

"I understand."

She nodded.

"I don't know who they were," she went on. "At the end, one of them stumbled and fell. The other helped him up. I only saw their faces for a moment, then they got into the plane. And then the shooting started."

She was a woman not easily understood or appreciated by

the world. She lived alone inside herself, happy except for the occasional loneliness that came when she remembered that she had no one to share her dreams with. She looked at Carter as if she'd found a soulmate.

"This is important," he told her gently. "What did they look like?"

"South Americans, I think," she said without hesitation. "Or Mexicans. They had that Indian look to them. But ninety percent of the people down there have Indian blood in them, so I'm not sure that's important. Does it help?" She wanted to help, her eyes said, to help *him*.

"It helps a lot," he said.

"Then you'd better leave."

He heard the distant sounds of confusion and the gathering of a mass of people.

"Harry's over there asking Ron questions," Edie said, pointing back at the mechanic who had directed Carter to the fueling area. "Harry's in charge of security tonight. He looks pretty mad."

Harry was the security guard Carter had talked with in the terminal. Harry listened to the mechanic Ron, then nodded and glanced at Carter. His heavy face was growing ruddy with an old rage recently refueled.

"Your CIA badge is fake," Edie said. "But I don't care. I know you couldn't do anything bad."

Carter grinned.

"Thanks," he said. "I try."

He kissed the cheek that smelled faintly of Ivory soap and slipped into the shadows beside her. There was only one explanation for Harry's appearance. Security had found the jet with the miniguns, and Harry had connected the jet to the stranger from the FAA asking questions.

Carter slid along the fueling area's shadows, watching the security chief march to Edie. She talked to him, her fingertips stroking the cheek were Carter had kissed her. Her eyes were dreamy, and a small smile curled her lips.

Uniformed airport police and plainclothes guards emerged

on the tarmac from different entry points. Some effort had been put into organizing them.

Carter moved through the shadows while the security force spread out. Harry shouted at some of them, gesturing that they go in various directions.

Carter circled silently until he came to the end of the shadow of a long building. Across from him was a wide-open space of lighted tarmac. Harry stood in the center. Beyond the former hockey star were more shadows that would lead Carter back to the Westwind jet.

Harry surveyed the searching men, hands on his barrel hips. He was an obstacle on flat feet.

An airport policeman walked by Carter, so close that Carter could smell garlic from the man's Italian dinner. The gun he wore in the holster at his side glowed black and lethal. Carter backed softly into the densest part of the shadow, flat against the building, silent and still.

The man passed, the garlic trailing him like a dog.

Carter watched all the men, waiting for the moment when their eyes were busy elsewhere, their backs turned.

When that split second came, he dashed soundlessly with the speed of an antelope. He was the premier Killmaster, with the accomplished skills and knowledge that all men are capable of but few are willing to achieve. He had the extraordinary drive to set himself above all others.

Carter slapped a hand over Harry's mouth.

He grabbed his arm and dragged the former athlete into the next path of shadows. The guard struggled, smart enough to use his sagging heaviness as a weapon.

He threw himself back against Carter.

Carter used his legs as springs and pushed Harry against the rough wall.

"I don't have a gun," Carter hissed. "And I'm not going to kill you or anyone here."

Harry's eyes were wild with fury. His breathing was labored with frustration. The aroma of Sen-Sen hung like a cloud around his head.

"If I let you go, will you shout?" Carter rasped.

Harry growled deep in his throat. Then he ripped an arm loose and violently bashed Carter's chest.

"Sorry, Harry," Carter said, breathing hard. "You blew it."

He slammed a fist into Harry's double chin. Harry's head snapped back against the wall. The limp body slid down like melting wax to the tarmac. Licorice smells drifted up.

Carter looked around.

The guards were still busy carrying out Harry's orders. If Harry had been more rational and less emotional, he'd be back out on the tarmac now, diverting his men so Carter could slip back to the jet and get on with his mission.

Carter sighed and moved stealthily through the shadows. Away from the fueling area, the smell of gasoline and grease grew stronger. Water dripped from an outside faucet. Oily rags were piled in a plastic bucket ready to be discarded. Carter moved on. The buildings were a series of squares and rectangles with occasional splotches of light. Only a few security men had investigated this far. Those few stepped into the shadows and quickly out again; they had too much territory to cover.

At last Carter stopped at the edge of another building.

Ahead was Carter's Westwind jet—guarded by three armed airport police.

Nick Carter walked into the open space toward the three young policemen. They were doing their jobs, loyal and brave Americans, and Carter was proud of them. But because of AXE's need for secrecy, he couldn't tell them who he was. And if he didn't, they might, in the line of duty, kill him.

"Halt!" one of them cried out.

"All right, men," Carter said cheerfully as he continued walking. "Who knows karate here?"

"What?"

The three youthful police leveled their rifles at him.

"Who are you?" asked one.

"Identification!" another barked.

"I'm impressed," Carter said, pleased. "But it's important to know martial arts, too. You might run into someone like me."

Carter broke into a run.

The policemen's fingers were on their triggers.

Carter ran zigzags.

"Pay attention!" he shouted.

The young officers looked at one another, puzzled, not willing to shoot yet, worried about the unarmed man running crazily on the tarmac.

Their fingers flexed.

"Feet!" Carter shouted.

"What?"

He leaped and sliced a foot into one young man's chin, knocking him flat and unconscious.

The other two pulled out their billy clubs.

"Hands!" Carter yelled.

He spun and chopped the flat of his hand into the second man's neck.

The policeman's eyes rolled up and he pitched over, also out cold.

"Elbows!"

Carter swung back his elbow in a lethal punch that only grazed the chin of the last man.

Carter turned, surprised.

The young man had ducked. Now he crouched, his eyes warily on Carter. He crab walked backward to the jet's door. Still protecting, following orders.

"You learn fast," Carter complimented him. "You've got stamina and good reflexes."

The policeman pointed his rifle at Carter.

"This time I'll shoot!" he warned.

Carter nodded. He knew the guard would.

And he turned as if to walk away.

"Be sure to get some advanced karate lessons," Carter advised.

Then he lunged back toward the young man in a somersault and rolled forward.

"Head!" Carter shouted.

Shots spit into the tarmac.

Carter came up and glimpsed the surprised eyes of the young policeman.

Then he butted headfirst into a hard stomach. He stood up and let the immobilized youth drop, the wind knocked out of him.

Carter pressed his fingers against the boy's neck artery, stopping the blood to the brain just long enough for unconsciousness to set in. He'd sleep for awhile.

Once the boy was out, Carter stood up and looked around at the open space in front of the jet. No one was near. His Killmaster's luck had held. Still, he knew that luck was just a fantasy. He made his own circumstances. He had knocked out all three young men in less than two minutes. He hoped it had been a lesson for them: get more training or find a different line of work.

He dragged them one by one away from the jet, climbed in, and started the engines. He knew what his next stop was.

SEVEN

The Westwind rose in the air like a giant bird, circled over Philadelphia, and flew southwest above the twinkling nighttime earth. When Carter was on course, he picked up the microphone and said the code words into the jet's radio that would connect him to Hawk.

"I hope I didn't wake you, sir," Carter said, listening long-distance to the sudden explosion of air that told him Hawk had just lit another cigar.

"Not this time," Hawk's voice said gruffly.

"I'll be quick." Carter told Hawk of the happenings at the Philadelphia airport.

"Good work, N3. More Indian faces, eh?"

"Keeps reminding me of Itzamná, the Mayan god.

"I'll run a check on other airports—see if anyone else had trouble night before last," Hawk said, puffing in the distance. "Where are you off to now?"

"New Mexico."

"Good hunting!"

Duane Michaels's abandoned Gulfstream turbojet sat squashed and brittle on the New Mexico desert. Scattered sage and junipers surrounded it on the rough sand a hundred miles north of Santa Fe, not far from the Ojo Caliente River where Tiger Santos—or another pilot—had landed and left the jet.

Already vandals had pulled out the seven passenger seats, ripped wiring in the cockpit, stolen the controls, and unscrewed nuts and bolts to take off the turbojet's soft tires. One tire lay on its side, waiting to be picked up whenever the vandals returned.

Carter went back to his Westwind jet for Wilhelmina. He already carried Pierre and Hugo, and now he felt complete. Desert vandals could be teenagers looking for thrills, old women looking for food, or scavengers with guns, a need for money, and an absence of morals. This vandalism looked like scavengers.

Wilhelmina securely holstered under his arm, Carter walked back to the jet. Eventually Michaels's Gulfstream would be completely stripped, its carcass left to a long future with little decay and less interest on the lonely desert.

He searched through the litter inside the jet. The air was dry and stuffy with the faint odor of dust brought in by the boots of earlier searchers. Torn wall paneling, chair stuffing, magazines, and Albany restaurant bills for Michaels's business associates littered the floor. Carter sifted through the mess, impressed that the FAA had discovered the map fragment of southern Mexico amid the rubble.

He found nothing of interest on the floor and worked his way back along the walls to the cockpit. He ran his hands over the instrument panel, checked inside the holes where wiring and expensive navigational devices had been ripped out, and finally squatted on the debris to survey the chaos—and think.

In the distance he heard the pickup. He walked outside, Wilhelmina ready at his side, into the ancient land of the Anasazi Indians. Far off, the speeding pickup hurled clouds of yellow and brown sand into the desert air. As it approached, Carter saw four modern cowboys waving bottles of tequila and riding the pickup as if it were a bucking bronco and each were a rodeo star.

The pickup tore across the gray and brown desert, ripping up the rock and cobble borders that the Anasazi had built by hand centuries ago into troughs to catch the desert's rare rainwater. Five hundred years ago, the Anasazi had made the arid wilderness bloom with corn, squash, beans, and berries. The Indians had carved pueblos with thousands of rooms into the faces of sheer cliffs. They developed astronomy and highly artistic forms of pottery, and spread their culture over New Mexico, Arizona, Utah, and Colorado. In those days, more people lived in some parts of southwestern Colorado than did now.

Carter reflected on this as he watched the whooping cowboys approach in the sand-eating, trough-destroying pickup. Two sat in the cab, and two were in the truck bed in back. The quartet guzzled their tequila and shouted their laughter into the pristine desert air. They had money to burn, and they wanted more. These four weren't really cowboys—people whose spirits were nurtured by land and animals—but vultures waiting for death to feed on. Three rifles and a shotgun stuck out at different angles from the pickup, casually threatening any who might cross them. They'd come back to Michaels's jet to see what else they could steal to sell.

When they noticed Carter's jet, they whooped with drunken delight. Their attention riveted, they sped up to the new prey, stopped in a hail of sand and gravel, and leaped out carrying their guns. Carter retreated under the wing of the Gulfstream to observe.

"Another one!" cried a short stocky man. He threw his battered Stetson to the ground and jumped up and down. "Hot damn!"

"All ours!" shouted a second.

The second man was of medium height and weight, his grimy red bandanna knotted so tightly around his throat that it bobbed with his Adam's apple.

"Dope!" yelled a third. "Maybe there'll be dope this time!"

The third had long sandy hair pulled back untidily with a rubber band. Dirt stuck to the hair, a glaze of brown grease. He threw his arm across the shoulders of the second man, and they gazed with anticipation at Carter's jet.

While the first man danced in the sand around his Stetson, the fourth man stood silent and weaving, holding a shotgun in one hand and a half-full bottle of tequila in the other. He looked at the jet much as a cannibal does at an unexpected visitor during a famine.

"Want to sell yours?" Carter asked, stepping away from the Gulfstream. Greed had worked with Michaels; it should work with these clowns. Greed, unfortunately, was reliable.

"Hey!"

"Who's that?"

The four men spun around, their eyes narrowed. The quartet were all in their late twenties and early thirties, still strapping with the remains of youthful muscle. But they were old enough to have been around, their cagey faces said, and experience was a painful teacher.

Carter patted the Gulfstream's wing.

"Know it's not much," Carter went on casually about the wreckage, "but I'm in the business of refurbishing jets for executives. This one would sure look good once it was fixed up again."

The men glanced at one another.

"How much're you offerin'?" the fourth man said, the tequila and shotgun dangling at his side. The oldest, he looked suspiciously at Carter's Luger.

"It's worth a lot!" the one with the bandanna assured Carter.

"Damn right!" said the one with the ponytail.

Now that Carter had their attention, he had to offer enough to get what he wanted.

"How does twenty thousand sound?" Carter suggested.

"Dollars?" The youngest man scooped up his Stetson from the ground, whirled it around his hand, then plopped it on his head. "We're rich!"

"Now wait a minute," the oldest one said. "What's the catch?"

"No catch. Straight deal," Carter went on, cradling the

Luger across his arm. "Just let me see the ownership papers."

The four men's faces drooped with unhappiness. Even the suspicious face of the oldest man was deeply disappointed. The jet wasn't theirs to begin with, but with amazing speed they had forgotten that little detail. The proper amount of incentive can make any desire seem like an accomplished fact.

"Too bad," Carter said sympathetically. "Guess I'd better look for the salvagers then."

"Salvagers?" the oldest one said, his eyes growing wily with possibilities.

"Sure. You know the law of salvaging," Carter said, thinking fast as he made up a rule to fit the situation. "If the owner abandons something for three days on open land, whoever finds it first and takes possession, owns it."

The men were saved.

"That's us!" yelled one.

"We were here first!" shouted another.

"Can you prove that?" Carter asked, his turn now to be suspicious. "Twenty thousand's a lot of money."

Suspicion was something they understood.

"We saw each other!" the youngest man said. "That's our proof!"

"Sorry," Carter said, shaking his head. "I don't know you."

"We're the Shews," the oldest man said, pushing the youngest aside. "I'm Dan Shew and these here are my brothers." He waved the hand with the tequila bottle in an arc to include the others. He was their leader, too, and intended to keep the position. "Come over to visit now and again."

"You stripped this jet," Carter said.

"Salvaged," Dan Shew corrected. He smiled, showing broken teeth and some intelligence. "It was just lying around. Not good for much otherwise."

"Danny tried to start it up," the brother with the bandanna said proudly.

"We work around here," Dan Shew continued methodically. He dealt with one issue at a time. "Fences, hauling, like that. We decided to work on the plane, too."

"Tell him how you tried to make it go, Dan. Go on! Tell him!" The brother with the bandanna nodded encouragement.

"Shut up, Ronnie," Dan said without looking at him.

"Did you see the pilot when you got here?" Carter asked.

"I was the only one that saw him," Dan Shew said. "I came alone the first time. And don't you try to tell him any different!" Dan Shew glared at his brothers. They dropped their gazes guiltily. "That's better," he told them. "It was a Mex," he said to Carter. "A pretty Mex in dime-store clothes. You know, all dressed up?"

"A shiny black jumpsuit?" Carter suggested.

"Yeah. That's it."

"What did you do when you got here?" Carter asked the oldest brother.

"Nothing," Dan Shew said and grinned. "Never had no plane land here before. I just watched. The Mex gets out and stands by the plane for a while. Pretty soon a Navy jet lands too. The Mex talks to the pilot, and they have some kind of argument. Then they both get into the plane and it roars off."

"*United States* Navy?" Carter asked.

"Sure. What I said."

"They talk to you?"

"Naw. It was like I wasn't even here. They were arguing about where to go. The Mex wants to go to Chiapas. The pilot's not sure, says he's got to hit San Antone first."

"A U.S. Navy pilot?"

Dan Shew considered.

"Guess not," he said at last. "Another Mex, and he's got jeans and a T-shirt on. None of the regular pilot stuff."

"So Tiger Santos got out," Carter mused thoughtfully. "And with a Navy jet."

"You know," Dan Shew went on, "I didn't steal nothin'. Went on home, told the boys all about it. Next day I come back, and there's soldiers in uniforms all over the place. Didn't come back again until that afternoon. Then everybody was gone, just me and my brothers here. Us and the plane. All I wanted to do was fly it." Dan Shew drank from his bottle and staggered. Two of the brothers propped him up.

"Thanks." Carter walked past them, toward his Westwind.

"What about our twenty grand?"

"I'll mail it to you," Carter said, "in care of the plane you wrecked."

"Salvaged!" the brothers chorused.

"Send it to the El Rito post office!" the youngest brother decided.

Carter got into the Westwind.

"Well, so we took a few things from the plane, sure!" Dan Shew called out. "Might as well. We needed the money for important stuff. . . ."

Carter closed the door. From the cockpit, he watched the brothers and started the motors. Their faces were slack with hungry stupidity. He taxied the Westwind across the New Mexico desert, junipers and sage catching at the plane's wheels and wings, then lifted off.

EIGHT

Nick Carter flew south into Mexico, a country Hernán Cortés reportedly described by crumpling a piece of paper to illustrate the mountains that crown two thirds of the land. The Mexican state of Chiapas, Tiger Santos's destination, is far south, bordering on Guatemala, and the people there are mostly Mayan Indians. The Maya, at the height of their civilization, built great temple complexes to honor their gods, and the most important of their gods was Itzamná— Itzamná, the name printed on the scrap of paper hidden under the wristwatch band of Carter's attacker in San Antonio and the name that appeared in a KGB report about Maxim Barkov, the KGB chief in Mexico.

Carter considered this as he headed toward Tuxtla Gutiérrez, the capital city of Chiapas, where there was an airport. Beneath him the Sierra Madre del Sur rolled and jutted, green and fertile with nature and the primitive farming of backbreaking Indian labor. The unique pueblos of the Anasazi and the majestic pyramids of the Maya had given the modern descendants of both tribes concrete gifts from their pasts. History can be consolation for the reduced present, and a hope for a better future.

Again Hawk was waiting for Carter's call.

"Norfolk, Atlanta, New Orleans, Houston, and San Antonio," Hawk said, his distant voice gruff with tension. "I don't like it. Too much geography involved. Apparently Santos stopped in each city. He must be more than a little crazy, all the shooting he does. We found a few witnesses who also saw one or two 'passengers' sneaking onto the jet at each stop. Far as we can tell, that's what Santos was doing in every city—picking up people. The purpose and ultimate destination are still mysteries.''

''Perhaps I can help you, sir,'' Carter said, then he told his superior what Dan Shew had overheard and seen in the New Mexico desert.

''You'd better get right down there to Chiapas,'' Hawk advised. ''Navy jets, eh?''

Carter smiled as he listened to Hawk puffing on one of his adored cigars in his office in the Amalgamated Press and Wire Services Building on Dupont Circle in Washington, D.C.

''I'm on my way,'' Carter said. ''Should land in an hour or so.''

''Navy jets!'' Hawk suddenly exploded. ''Christ!''

''Makes it too big an operation for drugs or black-market pharmaceuticals,'' Carter mused.

''I'm going to call someone at the Pentagon,'' Hawk muttered. ''I don't like this at all.''

''I'd like to know what Maxim Barkov's connection is to Itzamná,'' Carter said thoughtfully.

''MI5 has 'lost' the new decodings and translations,'' Hawk growled. ''Stuck in some computer somewhere between there and here. If it weren't so important, I'd laugh.''

Carter could hear him chewing on his cigar. Hawk's cigars were a source of consolation and celebration, depending on which emotion was more appropriate to the occasion.

''They'll locate it,'' Hawk decided. ''Probably have the wrong program file word for it. In any case, I'll find out and get you the information. But meanwhile, Nick, I want you to take care of yourself. Get those injuries seen to, then find out what the hell is going on in Chiapas!''

* * *

Nick Carter sat in the quiet, nighttime Chiapas airport bar and nursed a Dos Equis beer. He was tired and frustrated. He'd been through the airport—searched it and talked to personnel—but had found no sign of Tiger Santos or a U.S. Navy jet.

Carter got up abruptly and carried his briefcase through the restroom door marked *Men, Hombres,* and *Xib*—English, Spanish, and Mayan. Carter lay the briefcase across the sink and took a deep breath. He looked in the tile-framed mirror and saw the tiredness etched on his lean, rugged face. Suddenly the cheeks were gaunt, the eyes glazed.

He popped open the briefcase. No one else was in the cool, tiled restroom, so he stripped off his cotton shirt and peeled the bandages from his chest. The lacerations were healing rapidly, almost closed, with no sign of infection. Soon they would be only pale pink ribbons snaking across his chest, additions to his collection of scars. He swallowed some antibiotics and dabbed on more antiseptic, feeling the reassuring sting in the cuts. New, thinner bandages in place, he smiled in the mirror. Already he felt better.

Carter lathered soap onto his hands, and scrubbed his underarms, neck, and face. He rinsed with warm water, then splashed his face and neck with cold.

Chills spread up his spine. Vigor was returning to his face.

He put the simple white cotton shirt back on, brushed his thick dark hair, and returned his supplies to the briefcase. He stood back from the mirror, briefcase in hand, and looked at himself.

There was color in his tan face again, and a sparkle in his eyes. The hollowness was gone, replaced by a look of health and eagerness to live. He grinned at himself, pleased with the transformation, and swung out the door and back to his table in the bar.

The Dos Equis had a good bite to it. Carter drank and looked at a brilliantly painted Tree of Life that decorated the wall across from his table. The Tree of Life was a Bible in clay, telling in ornate, handmade figures the story of Adam and Eve. From the center of the tree, the traditional serpent stared out at him, but instead of its being sleek and evilly conniving, it was plumed and benign.

"*Una otra, por favor,*" Carter said to the bartender across the quiet room, raising his almost empty glass. He drained it and glanced at the four other customers spread around the small room.

The bartender nodded. He had a round face, straight eyebrows, and a shaggy haircut that caused his heavy dark hair to jut at strange angles. He glanced in the mirror at himself and smiled appreciatively.

As the bartender returned to work behind the bar, Carter watched a young woman with skin the color of café au lait saunter into the room. She swung up the bar, put one hip on a barstool, and leaned an elbow on the bar. She was posed in such a way that her slim hips, beautiful legs, and high round breasts were a glaring invitation.

It was a new reason for Carter to smile.

"Carta Blanca," the young woman said to the bartender.

He gave her a dazzling grin of white, square teeth that gleamed in his dark face. He patted his unruly hair, creating even more tufts that stuck out from his head.

"I've just come from Mexico City, and I'm thirsty," she told him in Spanish.

"It is a long flight," the bartender sympathized, hungry eyes on her. His Spanish had a slight Mayan accent.

The bartender pushed Carter's Dos Equis aside and pulled out a bottle of Carta Blanca. He popped open the lid and poured it into the glass he'd gotten for Carter's beer. He slid the glass with the golden Carta Blanca across the bar to the young woman.

"*Gracias,*" she said. "I've been waiting for this." She tipped the glass and drank.

As Carter watched her, the bartender got out another glass and brought the bottle of Dos Equis to Carter's table.

Carter readjusted his attention to the bartender.

"Is that Eve's serpent in the Tree of Life," Carter asked

him conversationally in Spanish, "or Kukulkán?"

The bartender's eyes had been wandering back to the woman at the bar, but now they returned to Carter with respect.

"You know about the old gods, *señor*?"

"Some. As I recall, Kukulkán is the name the Maya gave to Quetzalcoatl, the Aztec's feathered serpent god, when they incorporated him into their worship."

"That is correct," the bartender said and smiled. But he was losing interest.

"Eve's serpent didn't have feathers."

The bartender shrugged.

"Who is to say?" he said. "This is a land of the mysterious. Perhaps here the serpent does." He edged back toward the bar. "This is an old land, señor, and men and gods live long beyond their times."

The young woman was listening from the bar. Her long dark hair was pulled back and twisted at the nape of her neck. Her face's delicate bone structure gave her a refined beauty that was at odds with the seductive way she stood. She was after something.

"What about women?" she asked the bartender.

The bartender returned to his post behind the bar. He wiped the bar in front of the woman with an immaculate white cloth. He stared at her breasts while he worked.

"Men make history," he said. "Women are history. It is the natural way."

"It is our country's way," she said, putting her glass on the polished bar. "There's a difference between natural and cultural." She looked down into her golden beer. "I've been hearing stories about ghosts in the jungle south of here. I'm an archeologist. I've been working on the pyramid at Cuello in Belize. I've heard that there are some unexplored temples that are being used for old rites down south. I've been told that you know where I can find them."

The bartender whisked the white cloth from the bar and his eyes from her round, softly heaving breasts. He turned to wash glasses in the sink. His hands moved busily. He lifted a glass to see whether it was clean. He inspected it carefully, turning it from side to side in the light above his head.

"I don't know what you mean, *señorita*," he said. "I have work to do."

"Whole villages vanishing," she went on. "Strange gods or godlike people flying into the jungle."

The bartender shrugged and lifted a wet hand to smooth the wild hair on his head that he gloried in. He smoothed it as if to remove attention from himself.

She watched him silently, tapping her fingers on the bar, frustrated.

Carter picked up his Dos Equis and walked to the bar. He sat down beside her.

She looked at him, and he looked into her eyes. Her eyes were a deep blue, the color of lapis lazuli, and he smiled.

"Hello, Linda," he said in English. "You're new at this. Much too blatant. You've frightened him off."

"Nick!" she exclaimed in her soft Texas accent. "What are you . . ." She frowned, hairline creases forming between her dark brows. She seemed to shiver, then she gathered herself together and hopped off the barstool to leave.

Carter grabbed her arm and sat her back on the stool. She glared at him, angry.

Carter turned to the bartender while holding on to Linda.

"I admire your Tree of Life," Carter said casually in Spanish to the man behind the bar. "I'd like to buy it. Is it for sale?"

"They are sold all over the city," the bartender said, his back still to them.

"I'd like one just like yours. I'll pay you well."

The bartender shook his head.

"Go to the city. The Michoacán Shop."

"It would be more convenient to buy yours," Carter said, disappointed. "But I suppose if I must . . . I'll need directions."

The bartender gave them hurriedly, never once looking at Carter or Linda. Carter thanked him, pulled Linda to his table, picked up his briefcase, and took her out the door into the night.

Linda wrenched her arm free.

"Goddamn you!" she fumed. "You've ruined everything!"

"You've got a lot to learn," Carter said, amused.

She stalked off toward a dusty taxi. Carter followed her.

"German extraction," he said behind her back. "A Mexican citizen, but working for someone . . . perhaps the U.S. government?"

She walked faster and pulled open the taxi's door.

She whispered her destination to the driver, got in, and started to slam the door.

Carter grabbed it, slid in next to her, and closed the door quietly.

"Educated," he went on in English. "Probably working for the government. The President, perhaps?"

She sat back in the corner against the door, crossing her arms over her magnificent breasts.

"Get away from me. I don't want you. I don't need you." She held her head high and proud.

"You've come a long way from San Antonio," Carter observed.

"I was *working*!"

"Did you have to turn any tricks? You were so grubby back there that maybe you got away without having to. Unfortunately, you're going to have to get used to it. Part of the business for female agents."

She slapped his face.

He caught the hand in midair and laughed.

"Now that I've got you," he said and grinned, "I know just what I'm going to do with you!"

The taxi stopped in front of an old hotel built of stone. Blue and green tile bordered the large double doors and the windows of the flat, two-story building. Large wrought-iron lanterns sent light out onto the old paved street.

Linda threw money at the driver.

"My wife!" Carter told the driver in Spanish. "Sorry."

Linda snarled under her breath, got out of the taxi, and marched toward the hotel's double doors.

The driver followed her with his eyes, nodding and smiling as Carter slid across the seat to get out.

"She is high-strung, that one," the driver observed. "Be firm. She will respect you and give you many babies!"

Carter laughed again and followed Linda through the double doors.

"Get away from me!" she hissed.

"Wouldn't dream of it."

"I hate you!"

"You used to be impressed that I was a spy!"

"Screw you."

The clerk behind the registration desk stared at them.

Carter waved.

"Wife's a little peeved at me," Carter called to him in Spanish.

The registration clerk smiled, understanding, his pen suspended above the desk as he took in the excitement.

Linda stalked to him.

"This man is not my husband!" she announced. "He's annoying me. Get rid of him!"

Having given her orders, she turned, arrogant as a queen, and walked haughtily to an old-fashioned elevator set in a wrought-iron cage.

Carter went to the desk and got out his wallet.

"Guess we've both had too much to drink," he explained and smiled. "Send two good dinners up. Steak, corn, fruit. A bottle of champagne. The best you have." Carter winked and handed the clerk fifty dollars.

The clerk dropped his pen and slipped the money into his trouser pocket. He was savvy and hoped to have more sophisticated guests who could afford to be accommodated.

"Of course, *señor*," he said smoothly. "Will there be anything else?"

The old elevator hummed, carrying Linda up.

"Better give me a key. She'll probably lock me out."

They laughed and watched the elevator disappear. In Latin countries, a woman is to be tamed—even a wife—when she is young and beautiful.

"I understand completely, *señor*!"

Carter watched the clerk pull a key from the pigeonhole marked 2C.

"*Gracias*," Carter said and saluted. He marched to the stairwell, feeling better than he had in days.

NINE

The Tuxtla Hotel room was large and airy. The window was open, and a cool mountain breeze blew against an old overstuffed chair. There were wooden night tables on either side of the wrought-iron double bed, a carved table that held a clay water pitcher and glasses, and an overhead light suspended beneath a slowly rotating ceiling fan. The bathroom door was closed. Carter shut the room's door behind him and locked it.

He heard running water from the bathroom. A small stream, probably the sink. Carter sat in the comfortable chair and looked out the window across the city. He thought about Mexico's weath: more oil than Saudi Arabia, more natural gas than the United States, and fertile land for farming corn, wheat, cotton, and bananas. Still, the nation's capital—Mexico City—had grown into the largest city in the world, unwieldy with peasants trying to escape the poverty of rural areas only to find new poverty in the concrete bungalows built like cereal boxes on the outskirts of the city. Without resources, a country couldn't provide food and work for its people. But even with resources, it often couldn't do the job. Still, Mexico tried. Inflation had slowed, and the peso was regaining strength. The government was returning land to the peasants and teaching them to work it more productively.

There was an air of contemporary optimism to the country; people truly wanted to push the past into an exciting future.

Carter heard the stream of water in the bathroom stop.

He got up and walked softly to the door.

The knob turned.

Carter flattened himself against the wall.

Linda came out, still in her dress and pumps, smelling of an old-fashioned rose water, a toothbrush in her hand. She crossed the room to the bed where her suitcase lay open.

Carter slipped inside the bathroom and turned on the bathtub's taps.

"Who's that?" Linda yelled and ran to the bathroom. "What are you doing?"

Carter whisked her up and threw her over his shoulder.

"I've wanted to give you a bath since I first saw you in San Antonio," he said.

"Stop it!" she yelled, beating her fists against his shoulder blades.

He laughed and carried her to the bed.

"Get out of here! Help! Help!" she screamed.

Carter dumped her onto the bed.

"No one's going to help," he said. "The hotel clerk has fifty dollars that says we're married."

He rolled her over and unzipped the back of her dress. She struggled like a salamander and wiggled across the bed.

"I don't need a bath!" she wailed. "I've got work to do!"

"We'll go to the Michoacán Shop tomorrow morning," he promised her. "First thing."

He sat her up and pulled the dress down over her shoulders. She popped up from the bed and ran to the door, the dress crumpled around her waist.

"You can't get away." he said, grabbing her around the hips.

"This is rape! Help! Help!"

"If I can't undress you, you'll go in as you are."

She kicked him as he picked her up to carry her into the bathroom. Her feet pummeled his side until her pumps fell off. He peeled off pantyhose and bikini underpants, the fabric thin and fragile. She was pale under her clothes; some sort of dye had been applied to exposed parts of her body so that she would look more Mexican.

He felt her pause in her struggles, felt her confusion. Carter counted to three and dropped her into the bathtub.

"I hate you!" she screamed, water splashing up into her face, plastering her hair to her head, splashing over the side and soaking Carter's Gucci loafers.

Dye ran from her hair down her face and into the bath water.

"You're a mess," he announced. "You really do need a bath."

She looked at herself, at the brown water sluicing down her wet bra and dress. She held up her hands and saw them paling as if she didn't recognize them under the artificial color.

"Oh, my God. You've ruined me!"

"Not yet, my dear."

But she didn't protest as he pulled her dress over her head, and she unhooked her bra herself. He tossed the soaking clothes into the sink, got down on his knees, and leaned over the tub. He turned off the spigots.

She sat quietly, a child with large eyes, as he lathered soap onto a white washcloth.

"Is the water warm enough?" he asked gently.

She nodded.

"Close your eyes," he said.

She closed them, and he washed her face, carefully soaping the straight nose, the sculpted cheekbones, the broad, intelligent forehead, and the lips shaped as delicately as flower petals.

She sighed and he rinsed her face. The skin was almost alabaster with just a faint tinge left from the dye.

"You are very beautiful," he said.

"Thank you."

"Lean over."

She leaned forward, and he shampooed her hair with the

soap. It sudsed brown. He rinsed and washed it three times until at last her own golden color shone through like the sun.

"Stand up," he said.

As she stood, the water ran from her like a fountain. She had a tiny waist that flared downward into slim hips framing a golden triangle of soft hair. Above the waist were high, full breasts, suspended against her ribcage like birds in flight.

He lathered the washcloth and scrubbed her legs, her arms, her back, her hips, her flat belly, her round, soft breasts. She watched him with hot eyes.

When he was done, he breathed deeply.

"Sit down and rinse off," he said.

"In this water?"

She stared at him, pulling him to her with her eyes, and he forced his gaze down to notice the muddy brown water.

"Right," he said and pulled the plug.

When he looked up, she was still watching him. She cocked her head, questioning.

As soon as the water drained out, he put the plug back in and turned on the spigots.

"May I sit down now, please?" she asked politely.

"If you like."

She sat, and the water slowly rose around her, over her downy pubic hair, over her waist, up to her breasts that floated with the ebb and flow of the clean water.

"I didn't recognize you tonight," she said. "In the bar."

"You haven't had the training yet."

"You're dressed so differently. You were a cowboy in San Antonio. If I hadn't been told to watch for you, I would've thought you were just another dirty cowboy."

He grinned.

"I wanted to go to bed with you then," she murmured.

"And now?"

She looked up.

"I'm thinking about it," she said.

Carter roared with laughter.

She blushed crimson, angry, and scooped up some water and threw it in his face. He laughed harder, and she rose from the water like a virago, splashing him, pulling at his shirt buttons, tugging at his belt.

He picked her up.

She grabbed a towel and bit his neck.

He carried her toward the bed.

She wrapped her legs around his waist. He stopped beside the bed, stood legs spraddled, and held her ass tight against his belly. She panted, staring into his eyes as she toweled herself off.

Carter stood Linda on the bed and stripped off his clothes, then pulled her back to him, kissing her shoulders, her throat, her ears. Her hips moved, slightly at first, then more insistently. Her eyelids lowered, lost in desire. He snatched the towel away. He kissed her lips and swallowed the sudden burst of moisture. Her tongue eagerly explored his mouth.

His hands moved up to the beautiful high breasts. She slid down his belly, leaving a trail of heat. He seized her hips and thrust into her, and she moaned. And they made love standing next to the old wrought-iron bed in a room full of fresh mountain breezes.

When the knock on the door came, they were lying in bed, Linda's head buried in Carter's shoulder, half asleep.

"Hmmm?" Linda sighed.

"I'll get it," Carter said drowsily and smiled.

It was their dinner, rolled in by a deferential waiter who kept his eyes modestly lowered.

"By the window, please," Carter told him in Spanish. He held a towel wrapped around his hips.

The waiter nodded and pushed the old mahogany cart beneath the window. He left for the hall and returned again with two hand-carved mahogany chairs. These he placed on either side of the cart. He struck a match and lit three candles set in an ornate brass candelabra in the center of the cart. Next he pulled out a silver bucket of ice from the bottom shelf of the cart. In the ice bucket was a chilled bottle of California champagne.

"Would you like me to open it, *señor*?" the waiter asked,

his gaze glued to the hardwood floor.

"I'll take care of it. *Gracias.*" Carter handed him a crisp five-dollar bill.

"Muchas gracias, señor!" the waiter said, feeling the bill with his thumb and forefinger. *"Muchisimas gracias!"* He dropped the bill inside the band of his white trousers and bowed low. "We of the hotel wish you health and long lives!"

As the waiter bowed his way to the door, he lifted the side of his head and glanced at the bed. Linda grinned at him. A shy smiled spread across his Indian face.

"And please thank the registration clerk for us," Carter said.

The waiter nodded and sidled out the door, beaming. People of all cultures enjoyed the vicarious thrill of bringing two lovers together.

When the door closed, Linda jumped out of bed.

"I'm starved!"

She started for the table, then realized she was nude. She grabbed the sheet and wrapped it around her. Carter held a chair for her, then slid it beneath her to the cart.

"Aren't you going to put something on?" she asked as she lifted food covers and put them on the floor.

"Would you feel more comfortable?" he said and sat naked in his chair.

"Nope!" She dropped her sheet, and her porcelain breasts swung over the steaming food. "Let's eat!"

Carter rubbed his hands. It had been days since he'd had time for a good meal.

"I really messed up at the airport bar, didn't I?" she said as she cut her steak.

"Too direct," he said. He slathered butter on his ear of corn. "Sex and direct questions work sometimes, but not always. It's much better to get the person to feel safe. Fit yourself into their way of thinking, then invite them to give you information."

"You're a Killmaster, aren't you?" she asked, chewing thoughtfully. "That's tops."

"It's a challenge," he admitted. The corn was good, so fresh it must have been picked at sundown.

"You're a challenge," she said, laughing. "Oh, God—I feel so good! Be careful I don't fall in love with you!"

He looked over his ear of corn into her spectacular blue eyes. Suddenly shy, she gazed at her food and concentrated on eating. He watched her smooth face, vibrant with sexual satisfaction. She was impatient, eating the food as if it were the best and last meal of her life. She did everything with eagerness, almost as if she always wanted to be one jump ahead of where she was.

"You're too impatient," he told her. "Life comes in morsels, not gulps."

"I have too much to learn and too little time to learn it," she explained. She looked up and smiled, then returned to her meal. "Will you teach me?

He ate his steak. It was a cut of meat unknown to him. Each country had its own way of butchering. This meat was tender and delicious.

"What are you doing here?" he asked.

"The President's not sure what's going on down here. There have been some strange tales coming back to his ears." She put down her knife and fork. "He's aware of the foreign agents in Mexico. Either he didn't know you'd be here, or he didn't tell me." The last was a question.

"No one knows I'm here."

"Good," she said and nodded. "It has something to do with the Cuban you were chasing. Something to do with the Indians down here, too. Does Itzamná mean anything to you?"

Carter shrugged.

"A Mayan god," he said.

She watched him.

"You're too casual," she decided. "You know that Itzamná is a code word or something more." She grinned. "How's that for improving my techniques?"

He had to laugh.

"Much better."

"So why are *you* here?" she asked, and picked up her knife and fork again.

"The same as you. Trying to find out exactly what's going on." He told her about Tiger Santos's trip through the United States picking up secretive, dark-clothed figures.

She was thoughtful.

"Doesn't make much sense to me yet," she said. "Do you think they were fugitives who had to leave the country?"

"Maybe. Or maybe they were simply bringing something into Mexico."

She sighed.

"Oh, well. I guess it's our job to find out what's going on."

He shook his head. She had a refreshing way of assuming victory. She had yet to learn the price of it.

"We'll start at the Michoacán Shop tomorrow." She set her fork and knife down again. Her plate was clean. "When are we going to have the champagne?"

He grinned at her.

"Later."

She stared into his eyes, then pulled him toward her with a sudden flare of desire. She ran her fingers up his arm and touched his lips.

"Aren't you finished yet?" she asked softly. "Please hurry."

He ate, watching her, as she seemed to melt into the chair. At last he stood, and she rose to meet him. He pulled her against him, her thighs satiny and hot. He drew her head back and kissed her.

"I want to go to bed," she murmured. "Now!"

He picked her up, carried her across the room, and placed her gently onto the bed.

"Come here," she whispered huskily. "Again and again."

TEN

Far from the world of the assembly line, the Michoacán Shop nestled among other small shops in a cramped street of whitewashed stucco buildings. Before each doorway was a potter or weaver or silversmith. All were at work already, the dawn turning the sky a dusky rose on the horizon, the bite of night's mountain coolness still in the air. Some of the artisans sang melodies as old as the crafts they worked. Others had steaming bowls of thin gruel beside them, alternately eating and working.

The woman before the Michoacán had grizzled gray hair and a face whose downturned lines spread like a river across it. Two fat braids intertwined with red wool hung from her head. Her hands worked quickly, shaping flowers, birds, and stars.

She looked up and smiled at the *norteamericanos*.

"Do you like them?" she asked in Spanish. "See, I line them up so." She pointed to a row of newly made clay figurines. "When I am done, I can sit back and look at them. They make me feel good, here." She tapped her plump chest.

"I like them," Linda said. "The details."

The woman smiled, her crinkled face glowing with the praise.

Nick Carter looked at the Tree of Life behind her and through the doorway at more of various sizes.

73

Carter gestured at the large tree behind her.

"Do you make these?" he asked. "I saw one similar to that one at the airport."

She nodded, pleased.

"These will go on the next one," she said and gestured to the row of figures in the dust before her. "But that one at the airport was special."

"The serpent?" Linda asked.

"Kukulkán," the old woman said, nodding. "More and more the old gods are important."

"It was commissioned then?" Carter asked.

"I have many people far away who want them. They come with burros and carry them away south for villagers. Dieties cross all lines in our country."

"I'd like to buy that one for the Tuxtla Hotel," Carter said. He pulled out his wallet.

"Seventeen thousand six hundred pesos," the woman said, smiling. "No bargaining."

Carter did some quick arithmetic and handed her five twenty-dollar bills. She counted the money, folded it, and stuffed it down her bodice.

"A good start to the day," she said with a grin.

"If I were to look for them farther south, where would I go?" Carter asked as he picked up the Tree of Life.

"The jungle." The woman shook her braided head. "But it is very dangerous to those who do not know the ways."

"I'm an archeologist," Linda offered. "I've spent a lot of time in the jungle."

The woman shrugged heavy shoulders.

"Very well. It is east of here. Near the ruins of Bonampak."

Carter looked at Linda.

"I know the area," she said. "Treacherous."

"A few small villages," the old woman said, her lined face concerned.

"*Gracias*," Carter said.

He hoisted the Tree of Life above the dirt road, Linda took his arm, and they walked off.

"Beware the mysteries!" the woman called after them. "There is much magic in the jungle!"

Carter thanked her again, and he and Linda walked down the cramped street toward the center of Tuxtla Gutiérrez and their hotel.

"Are you really an archeologist?" Carter asked.

"I had a few courses in college," Linda said, "but archeology's too tame for me; the dead leaving adventure for the living."

"So what did you study?"

"Nothing. Everything. I didn't finish. I guess I'm restless. My stepfather knows the President . . . and so here I am. Gainfully employed."

"You do special jobs for the President?" Carter asked, surprised.

"This is my first. I like it . . . moving around . . . even San Antone. Except I had a hard time explaining to johns why I wouldn't take their money and go to bed with them." She shook her head and looked around the city. "I've always liked this town. There's a steadiness down here away from the glitter of a big city. Something to hold onto. An anchor. I don't know what it is exactly. I wish I did because I think it's important."

"You'd like that same steadiness inside you," Carter said softly.

"That's probably it. Maybe I'll find it someday."

They walked on past pink stone buildings and yards full of chickens. Dogs darted between them, their noses high and twitching. Dirty children with few clothes and fewer toys played along the road, pushing sticks in the dirt and knotting rags into ropes that they playfully threw around one another.

The day would be sunny and clear; the sky was already a deep blue.

The day shift clerk was puzzled but appreciative of Carter

and Linda's gift to the hotel of the Tree of Life. They set it up in the lobby, then took the rickety elevator to the second floor.

The men were waiting for them in the room.

Flat against the wall.

When Linda walked in, one grabbed her and threw her to the wrought-iron bed.

Instantly Carter pulled out Wilhelmina.

Another Luger smashed it from his hand.

Carter tackled a third man, slamming into his legs and knocking him over, then he jumped up and whirled around.

A 9mm Luger was pointing straight at his heart.

"Tie her up," the Cuban holding the gun ordered in Spanish.

The Cuban on the floor struggled to his feet, rubbing his legs. The other Cuban pulled the draperies from the window and sliced them into strips with his machete.

The Cuban with the Luger backed away from Carter.

"I remember your feet," he told Carter. "Stay back."

"San Antonio?" Carter asked.

The Cuban with the gun nodded curtly. He was a short, swarthy man with a large hooked nose and two fingers missing from his left hand.

"What do you want?" Carter asked.

"You, Killmaster," the Cuban replied sourly. "Only you."

It was late afternoon. The Mexican jungle was hot and humid, full of the tantalizing prospect of fever-carrying ticks and poisonous coral snakes. Nick Carter and the three Cubans rode a jeep along a rough path overhung with lush vegetation. Animals and birds made raucous sounds, then disappeared into the thick jungle before the jeep came into view. The men had been traveling for hours.

The three Cubans wouldn't talk. They sat in stony silence, rifles crossed over their arms. The one whose legs Carter had nearly crushed drove the jeep through the jungle wilderness.

They had traveled south first on the Pan American Highway and then had veered east on a dirt road that was probably only a map-maker's memory. The leader with the Luger sat next to Carter in the back seat of the jeep, Carter's briefcase braced between his ankles.

"A lot of unexplored Mayan ruins around here, I hear," Carter said conversationally.

The leader grunted and stared ahead at the primitive, winding road.

Time passed with the constant roar of the jeep's motor, the circling of the water bottle, and an occasional strip of wild boar jerky handed out.

It was twilight when the jeep turned off the road and bounced along a path so narrow that branches scratched the jeep. They drove through mudholes, the brown water splashing out of sight beneath the flat wide leaves and luxuriant dark flowers that rimmed the road.

Ahead, two torches were set on long poles in the ground. The jeep stopped in a patch of ferns, the torches' yellow light showing the wide mouth of a cave.

"Get out," the leader said curtly. "Over there." He pointed the Luger at the cave, where a tall, heavyset man stood below the entryway, a canteen in his hand. It was another Cuban, and by the arrogant way he stood, he was the real leader.

Carter stretched and walked toward him, the Luger held to his spine by the other Cuban. Carter hoped that at last he would learn something useful.

"Inside," the tall Cuban said. "Follow me."

Polychrome bits of pottery littered the entryway. Flat sedimentary rocks lay stacked by nature into walls on either side. They climbed twelve feet, scrambling over loose rock, into the torch-lit cave. In the center of the large cavern a cooking fire burned, and in it a large black iron pot set on stones bubbled. From the smell, Carter guessed it was some sort of stew. On the walls, figures with feathers, flattened foreheads, and ferocious eyes were painted in faded colors.

They were authentic Mayan cave paintings, perhaps a thousand years old.

Carter thought of Linda, missed her, but was glad the Cubans hadn't wanted her, too.

The tall Cuban with the canteen sat down on a boulder and gestured at another boulder beside him.

"At last, Killmaster." His voice wasn't pleasant.

Carter sat down. The aches from the bone-rattling ride were already disappearing. He looked around the cavern at the nearby pool fed by a shallow underground stream, at the stalactites dripping from the ceiling, at an old Indian who came to squat beside the cooking pot. The old man had wrinkles all over, even on his hands. He squatted about five feet away, his back to the boulders on which Carter and the Cuban sat, and stirred the stew that smelled of meat and vegetables. Carter watched the wrinkled hands.

"What were you doing in Tuxtla Gutiérrez?" the Cuban asked Carter. He had large liquid eyes, black and piercing. He kept them open as the threw his head back to drink from the canteen.

"Vacation," Carter said.

"Ha!"

The Cuban gestured to the old Indian.

"We'll eat now," he told him.

The old man picked up two chipped pottery bowls and dished out the stew. Carter counted seven Cubans, including the one he sat next to and the ones he'd seen outside and who now occasionally drifted into the mouth of the cave to look briefly at Carter and the Cuban. There appeared to be only the one Mexican.

"Killmasters never take vacations," the Cuban said. "Who or what is Itzamná?"

"The supreme Mayan diety," Carter said. "The inventor of writing and patron of culture and the sciences."

"Don't play games with me, Carter."

"So you don't know anything about it either," Carter said and smiled.

The Cuban hesitated, then gestured for the bowls of stew.

"You've had a long ride," he said. "We'll eat first, then talk."

"You haven't tried bribery yet," Carter suggested, still smiling. "Or torture."

"Old-fashioned, and often not effective."

The Cuban accepted the full bowl from the old Indian and handed it to Carter. Then he took the second bowl, blew across the top, and sipped.

Carter watched him eat. The old man had put nothing but stew into either bowl, but still Carter was cautious.

"Eat!" the Cuban commanded, licking his lips.

"Your bowl looks better than mine."

The Cuban glanced at Carter and shrugged.

"Very well."

They traded bowls.

The stew was heavily spiced and contained corn, chilies, beans, and chicken, as well as large hunks of potatoes, carrots, onions, and some other root vegetables that Carter didn't recognize.

"I'm sure you understand our interest," the Cuban went on thoughtfully. "Central America is important to us." He stopped eating and stuck up his thumb. "In Guatemala, the Indians side with Marxist freedom fighters against the government. In retaliation, the government death squads murder them . . . moderates, extremists, women, children, all! Only two percent of the people control two thirds of the farmland. It is outrageous!" The Cuban's eyes narrowed, and he stuck up his index finger alongside his thumb. "In El Salvador, it is much the same. Kidnappings, killings. Instead of your government allowing us to negotiate a compromise with the Salvadoran government, you insist on a military decision. For the present government! Against the Marxists! Not even a voice!" The Cuban stuck up his middle finger. "In Nicaragua, our Sandinista government must fight not only poverty and a shaky economy, but the old government gone into hiding and fighting now as guerrillas. Your government buys them guns and bullets, and they kill us!" The Cuban stuck up his ring finger. "Mexico! Here, in Mayan country, anything can happen. We know the United States is interested in the strange things going on here. They send their best man—Nick Carter. We know the KGB is interested. Maxim Barkov has been seen here repeatedly. And there are strange rumors of flying ghosts and odd events in the jungle.'' The Cuban dropped his hand and slapped his leg. ''If AXE and the KGB are interested, you know damned well we want to know what's going on too!''

The Cuban glared at Carter. Then, his irritation turning to hunger, he ate for a few minutes before speaking again.

''We are on the Guatemalan border here. The fight for freedom is just over the mountains.''

''Your brand of freedom isn't ours,'' Carter remarked.

The Cuban finished his stew and drank from the canteen.

''When was the last time Castro was elected to anything?'' Carter asked. ''He rules Cuba as if it were a fief and he were King George of England.''

''Our guerrillas fight with your weapons,'' the Cuban said, nestling the canteen between his legs. ''How do you think they got them? Stolen from the capitalist governments you supply. Without your guns, we wouldn't have a chance to win. Without your guns, so many people wouldn't be killed. On either side.''

Carter ate the last of his stew and set the bowl on the rocky ground.

''You're justifying your own aggression with ours. Is that logical?''

''We will win.''

''Maybe. But the cost will be high. And what will you be left with? Freedom for corpses is meaningless.''

''What did your Patrick Henry say? 'Give me liberty or give me death!' '' The Cuban sneered.

A sudden dizziness swept over Carter.

''Democratic capitalism is slow, but it works.'' Carter massaged his temples. ''Given a chance, the governments will feed the people, make jobs, give them a chance at longer, healthier lives.''

''Bullshit! They have had their chances and all they do is

work the peasants like slaves. They steal the land. Starve the people. The only thing that is working—growing—is their bank accounts!''

Carter desperately wanted to lie down. He squared his broad shoulders, but dizziness engulfed him. He swayed.

"Those were the old days,'' Carter mumbled. "Times have changed . . .''

The Cuban put a hand on Carter's back.

"Feeling ill, *compadre?*''

"I'm all right.''

Carter stood, needing to walk. He hoped walking around would shake off the nausea.

The Cuban stood beside him and took his arm.

"This way.''

He led Carter to a thin blanket. Carter could no longer focus. His knees buckled, and he collapsed onto the blanket beside the cooking fire. The old Indian grinned at him. Carter closed his eyes, then he jerked upright and struggled to his feet.

"Give in to it, *compadre,*'' the Cuban said. "It is an easy thing. Feel the goodness of it. You will go away inside, have important dreams.''

"The Mayan . . .''

Carter felt himself falling again. There was nothing he could do. The blanket was soft over the rock floor. The rock floor was soft, too, a downy bed.

"What was in the stew . . . ?'' Carter murmured from the floor.

The old man began to chant and sprinkled something wet over Carter. Carter's eyes fell closed.

"An ancient Mayan formula,'' the Cuban said. "From long before the time of the conquistadores.''

The dizziness was gone. Carter drifted into a land of pale blue and pink clouds. The clouds circled his feet, rose to his knees, and he walked lightly into emptiness.

"Itzamná,'' the Cuban said quietly. "Itzamná has called you here.''

Carter's throat itched with the need to talk. He pressed his lips together as his mind walked onward.

"You must tell me," the Cuban said. "You have no choice."

Carter nodded. He didn't want to nod.

"What else is happening in Chiapas?"

The old Indian's chant was rhythmic, lulling.

"Tiger Santos," Carter mumbled against his will. "Navy jets."

His mouth went dead. He couldn't feel it. In the clouds he saw the canteen. Thirsty. He walked toward the Cuban's canteen, saw him drinking from it all through dinner. The canteen! The canteen had to contain the antidote!

"Carter!" The Cuban's voice came from another world. "Carter! What else? Where is Tiger Santos?"

ELEVEN

Nick Carter's head was swollen to twice its size. He lifted numb hands and felt it. His fingers jerked away. The head was too tender to touch. He heard himself groan. Then cold silence. The scrambling of feet over loose rock.

Carter rolled over and opened slitted eyes.

The Cuban's canteen was by the boulder, next to Carter's briefcase.

He dragged himself there on his elbows, lifted the canteen, and poured brackish water down his furry throat.

The feet were padding toward him.

He grabbed the briefcase, opened it, and pulled out Wilhelmina.

"Save your strength, N3," the voice said, echoing in the empty cavern. A man's voice. English. An American accent.

"Who . . . ?"

"CIA. Philip Tice. Sorry I couldn't get here sooner."

Carter sighed and drank again from the canteen.

"What the hell happened to you?" Tice asked.

The cobwebs were clearing from Carter's swollen head. He opened his eyes wide and found himself staring at a bear of a man. Tice was probably six and a half feet tall, and must have weighed close to three hundred pounds, all of it muscle. He had pale blue eyes and sandy hair swept back thick and neat. Carter finished the canteen.

"Sandinistas?" Philip Tice wanted to know.

"Cubans," Carter replied, sitting up. His head whirled. He was groggy and felt as if he'd slept a week. "Hell of a way to get a good night's rest.

Tice smiled.

"You're a hard man to find," he said. "That girl Linda wouldn't talk until she was sure who I was. Then tracking you here . . . well, the Mayans aren't easy to buy."

"You came to rescue me?"

"That, and to get your help."

Carter stood and stretched. He swung his shoulders, then touched his fingers to his toes. His head had cleared and was back to its normal size, but he sat down again, still weak from the drug that had been in the stew.

"Why'd they leave you alive?" Tice wondered. "I'd just about decided I'd find you trussed up and dead."

"To make a point. They don't care whether I like them; they just want me to respect the rightness of their thinking. And they don't know what's going on down here. They probably figure I might be useful to them later. I'll be easier to find than someone they don't know."

"Makes sense," the CIA man said. "Hawk sends his regards."

"That's comforting."

Carter rubbed his head, and both men laughed.

"Does he always smoke those rotten cigars?" Philip Tice sat on the Cuban's boulder. He was dressed in camouflage pants and shirt, the brown and green zebra stripes making him look like an overgrown jungle plant.

"Long as I've known him. He says he likes them."

Carter pulled his own camouflage clothes from his briefcase. He stood and stripped off his silk trousers and madras shirt.

"What do you need help with?" Carter asked as he dressed.

"We're missing some cash. Enough to make us nervous. One million dollars, approximately."

Carter whistled.

"Headed for?"

"To fight the Communist rebels in Central America," Tice said.

"Figures."

Carter filled the Cuban's canteen at the shallow stream and attached it to his belt on the opposite side from where he'd carry Wilhelmina in a holster.

"You think Tiger Santos brought it in?"

"Yeah. Those people he was picking up were Sandinistas and Cubans. Exiles. They sidetracked the money on the way to the right hands. A bunch of moles, dammit. But our information is that the money never got to their regular rebel forces either. Word is that it's floating around here somewhere."

"And nobody knows why."

"Exactly."

"Then we'd better get going. You got a jeep?"

Tice stood, bandoliers across his shoulders swaying against his mountainous chest.

"You bet. Only way to get anywhere around here. I've heard there's something going on farther south. Want to give it a shot?"

Carter strode to the entrance of the cave. Morning light shone murky and thin through low gray clouds.

"Sounds like as good a place to start as any."

The rain began lightly, then quickly turned into a downpour. It ravaged the jungle leaves, whipping them into a froth of green. Nick Carter and the CIA man rode the jouncing jeep dressed in lightweight army ponchos, their heads covered against the torrent.

"When you're ready to switch," Carter said, "I'll drive."

Tice nodded. Ticks fell from the trees and slid down the men's ponchos onto the jeep's floor. Rattlesnakes, fer-de-lances, and coral snakes lay drowned on the pitted, muddy road. The jeep splashed and rumbled forward, crossing storm-created streams, bouncing around boulders moved by the rain onto the road. Tice slapped at his hands, flicking away ticks.

"Look out ahead!" Carter shouted.

An enormous tree lay across the road, its branches sticking out like spears to snare the unwary.

Tice hit the brakes, and the jeep skidded to a muddy halt.

Carter hopped out onto moss and waded forward. The tree was at least thirty feet long and four feet wide. Carter looked at it from tip to base and shook his head. The tip had fallen deep into the jungle, but the base. . . .

"Watch out! It's . . . !"

A spear suddenly quivered from the bark next to Carter's side.

He ducked and ran back to the jeep.

More spears and a few rifle shots hit the jeep as Tice leaped out. The two men crouched behind the vehicle. Arrows sang through the storm and splashed into mudholes around them.

"What the hell is this all about?" Tice growled to Carter.

"Sorry," Carter said. "I should've looked at the base first. Chopped by crude axes."

"Indians?"

"Them or someone who wants us to think they are."

Tice propped his M-16 on the jeep door, staying below with Carter, sheltered by the jeep. Two rifles fired from the jungle at the M-16. A spate of arrows landed around the agents. Then nothing.

"They don't have a lot of ammunition," Tice remarked.

"They'll try to circle us," Carter said.

"Why do they want us?"

"Don't know yet," Carter said. "Listen!"

They were silent. Only an occasional arrow shot through the storm at them. Thunder rolled far away. The rain pelted down.

"I don't hear anything," Tice said.

"They're moving," Carter whispered. "Breaking up into two or three groups. One's going to try to cross the road. You can hear them talking just under the sound of the rain.''

"I don't hear a damned thing," Tice said, irritated.

"There they go!" Carter said softly.

A group of young Indians in white shapeless garments and bare feet dashed ghostlike through the curtain of rain to the forest on the other side of the road.

Tice fired and got the last one in the thigh. The Indian kept running, the blood diluting to pink in the rain.

"Let's get out of here," Carter said. "I don't want to kill these kids.''

Arrows from their side of the road sailed through the rain at Carter and Tice. Carter opened the jeep door. Tice lunged in, Carter following quickly, but not before an arrow pinned together the front and back flaps of his poncho.

Carter started the jeep, keeping low in his seat.

"They could be renegades," Carter said. "They're losing their land, these jungle people. Some of them have turned to ambush and thievery to live.''

"But you don't think so," Tice said, squatting on the floor.

"They're just boys," Carter said, jerking the jeep into reverse.

Gunfire again rang in the air. The left front of the jeep dropped.

"They got a tire!" the CIA man moaned.

"Primitive, but not stupid," Carter said.

The jeep lurched backward. Clusters of arrows whizzed over their heads. More gunfire took out the remaining three tires. The jeep clunked on, back down the road.

Then another tree fell behind them.

Carter stopped the jeep.

"Damn!" Tice said. "We're cut off!"

"That does it," Carter said. "We've got no choice.''

He hit the brakes and peered over the left side of the jeep. Tice warily lifted his eyes over the right side.

"Watch out!" Tice called.

A long spear sliced through the rain over their heads. The

two men stared into the impenetrable jungle. The thick vegetation ran together like a solid green wall.

Then Carter saw the flash of wet brown skin.

He fired.

The body hurtled off a high branch into the muddy road. The boy bit his lips and held his shoulder where blood showed pink. He wore a quiver across his back. His bow lay twenty feet away.

Tice fired, and another Indian from his side of the road fell from the trees.

The first boy staggered to his feet and headed toward the bow. Carter fired in front of the boy's feet.

"Go back!" Carter shouted in Spanish.

The boy shook his head and staggered on.

A barrage of bullets thundered in the air. The boy looked around wildly. Bodies fell from the trees. The boy scooped up his bow and dashed into the jungle.

"Now what?" Tice growled.

No arrows or spears whined past them. No bullets shot at them. The gunfire that was concentrated in the jungle suddenly stopped.

"General Hilario Hiler's greetings!" a voice bellowed at the two men from the dense jungle in Spanish.

Tice looked at Carter.

"Sounds older, like a soldier," Tice said.

"Where are the Indian boys?" Carter shouted back.

"Ran away!" the voice yelled. "May we join you?"

"General Hiler?" Tice asked Carter.

"Mexican hero," Carter explained, then shouted again at the wall of jungle. "Keep your weapons in front of you!"

A dozen soldiers stepped from trees and bushes into the trough of mud that had once been a road. There were still five Indian boys in the road with various injuries. They moaned softly. Spears and arrows jutted at odd angles from the mud beside them. The rain beat down with new vigor.

"Thanks for your help," Tice said to the rangy lieutenant who led the soldiers toward them.

"We appreciate it," Carter said. "Have any medics?"

"Luis!" the lieutenant called. "See what you can do for the renegades."

The medic ran to an injured youth, opened a small kit with a red cross on it, and went to work.

"You are a hard man to find, Señor Carter," the lieutenant said.

"It's interesting that so many people are looking for me."

"The general wants to see you," the lieutenant went on. "It is a good thing he trained us to ride toward the sounds of gunfire. Otherwise, you would be dead." The lieutenant stared up at Tice's height as the two agents got out of the jeep. "Who is this?" he asked.

"Philip Tice, CIA," Tice said and stood like a majestic tree rooted to the spot.

"*Bueno*," the lieutenant said. "It might interest you to come along also."

"Where to?" Tice wanted to know.

"Monte Vista," the lieutenant said. "The general's ranch. He is waiting for Señor Carter."

"You think these Indian kids are renegades?" Carter went on thoughtfully.

The lieutenant looked at the wounded youths. Sadness filled his face.

"Logging, cattle, squatters," the lieutenant said, spreading his arms to encompass the area. "Our jungles grow smaller as Mexico grows larger. Some of our people live in remote tribes. They only know the jungle. When it gets cut down, they lose their homes. They have no food. They have nowhere to go, so they moved in on other tribes that are losing their lands themselves. It is inevitable. They become renegades. They cause a lot of trouble. Kill people. Get killed themselves." The lieutenant wiped a hand across his rain-drenched face. "Senseless."

Carter and Tice nodded.

"I will leave the medic," the lieutenant said and walked back toward the wall of jungle.

"You have a chain saw?" Tice called to him, gesturing at the two trees that blocked the road. "I think we can drive her if we can get her out."

The young lieutenant smiled.

"We ride!" he said. "Like the conquistadores! The horses are there." He gestured into the wilderness. "My general sent his best stallion for you, Señor Carter, but perhaps it would be better to carry this *gigante*!" The lieutenant grinned good-naturedly at Philip Tice.

Tice laughed and clapped the lieutenant on the shoulder.

"Don't worry, *hijo*," he told the general's man. "I can ride two at a time if I have to!"

Wielding machetes, soldiers with rifles slung over their backs cut through the tangled underbrush, and the lieutenant, Carter, and Tice followed. At last they reached a clearing where horses pawed the leafy duff and snorted the wet air.

At midafternoon the storm stopped, and the green jungle sparkled with rain suspended like diamonds on leaves and moss. Nick Carter, Philip Tice, the lieutenant, and the soldiers rode a high path pounded hard and clear by centuries of animals and humans. The jungle smelled of wet earth and rich vegetation. Bees and flies buzzed in the warm air. Parrots screeched. Steam rose and wavered like wraiths from the jungle floor.

"How much farther?" Tice shouted to the lieutenant ahead.

"A kilometer now!" the lieutenant yelled. "Maybe less!"

Tice patted the neck of the big roan stallion the general had intended for Carter.

"Your mother didn't feed you enough vegetables," he advised Carter.

"Your mother fed you too much spinach," Carter retorted, "and kept you out in the California sun too long."

They laughed, and the horses pranced forward. Carter, his briefcase across the saddle, rode an ebony stallion slightly smaller than Tice's. It had a leggy gait and excess energy coiled in its loins and shoulders. Two of the general's soldiers had doubled up so that Carter would have his own mount.

"So this General Hiler is a hero," Tice said. "Pull some information from that legendary encyclopedic knowledge of yours and tell me about him."

Carter laughed again.

"A real fighter," he began. "Asked to be assigned as a special observer for Mexico in both Korea and Vietnam. He saw a lot of action in both wars, unusual for his position and rank, but the general's a professional. He doesn't let anyone do his dirty work for him. Then, during Vietnam, his father died, and he returned to run the ranch. It's big—spreads over southern Chiapas and into Guatemala. An interesting man. Spent some time in a Mexican prison, too. Shot a rival in a love affair. Very Latin temperament. His wife had died in childbirth in the early sixties. Ten years later he fell in love with an actress in Mexico City. Alicia Piedra. She started seeing someone else secretly." Carter shrugged. "Hiler shot the lover and was going to Alicia Piedra's apartment to get her, too, when the police caught him."

"Has an old-fashioned code of honor," Tice mused.

"Add to that a fiery temper, wealth, and education, and you've got quite a man."

"How do you think he fits into this?" Tice asked quietly.

"Expect we'll find out soon. Stay loose. He's fought for the United States, but who knows what his politics are now."

The group rode around an immense bed of water hyacinths that extended in a white and green carpet. Long-horned tan and brown cattle sloshed through the flowered meadow in an irregular, slow-moving line.

"I grew up on a ranch in the Santa Ynez Valley," Tice said thoughtfully, his big frame rocking easily with the stallion. "In the spring there was a burst of California wildflowers that turned the mountains purple and orange. I went on roundups as a kid, mended fences, milked cows when the milker broke, fed the chickens and ducks, did every kind of chore imaginable. I always had at least one dog that followed me everywhere.'' Tice looked across the white hyacinths swaying in a light breeze. ''Sometimes I miss it.''

Nostalgia could be a useful emotion, Carter thought. It reminded one of the past so that future goals could be better understood.

''Maybe I'll go back someday,'' Tice said. ''My sister Marian runs the ranch, but I've got a share in it.''

The riders left the meadow of water hyacinths and rode their mounts up a steep hill that dropped over the crest into a gentle decline toward corrals and buildings. It was General Hiler's Rancho Monte Vista. Tice stared down, his light blue eyes feeding on the panorama.

An array of thatch-roofed huts nestled around a great hacienda built in a U-shape. Through corrals and ranch buildings, *charros* rode multicolored ponies, herding horses and cattle. The *charros* wore wide-brimmed hats and swung stiff lariats. In the distance, thin wisps of smoke rose from the jungle around the wide, flat hacienda and corrals. The Indians were out again after the storm with machetes, clearing the jungle in the ancient slash-and-burn farming technique to make room to plant corn, beans, and coffee.

The group rode down onto the plateau, between a short row of thatch-roofed *tiendas* sporting signs that said Coca-Cola, Fanta, and Pepsi. Indians stood in the doorways, drinking sodas and waving to the soldiers.

''Antonio! *Qué pasa*?'' a young woman in an embroidered skirt and blouse called to the lieutenant.

The lieutenant laughed and shrugged.

''*Nada*,'' he shouted. ''Nothing's happening.''

They rode on past children playing in the dirt, past soldiers drilling beside the corral that held extra work horses, past rain-wet clothes drying on the grass, and into the central courtyard of the impressive hacienda.

There, on the terra-cotta tiles of the central stairway, stood three people, one of them Linda. Her golden hair drifted around her shoulders in the light breeze. Her face was radiant with a shy smile directed at Carter.

As he dismounted with the other men, Carter smiled at her and shook his head.

In front of Linda stood a short, robust man built like a bronze bedspring. He smartly returned the salutes of his men. General Hilario Hiler. Behind him and next to Linda, holding her hand, was another woman of about Linda's age. She was shorter than the general, bronze and graceful in a flowing white *huipile* that fell below her knees.

"You found them, eh?" the general said in Indian dialect to the lieutenant. He was dressed in green fatigues, the press of his pants knife-sharp. There were no identification patches on any of the soldiers' uniforms.

"Yes, sir!" the lieutenant said and turned briskly to order the men to lead the horses for a cooling walk and rubdown.

Carter and Tice strode to the steps.

"Come in, Nick Carter," the general said. "Who is your friend here who rode my Diablo?"

Philip Tice introduced himself as they entered a spacious whitewashed room with thick dark ceiling beams. On a distant wall was a Tree of Life with the same feathered serpent Carter had seen in Tuxtla Gutiérrez. Another wall held photographs of Emiliano Zapata and Pancho Villa around a banner proclaiming the 1910 revolutionary cry, "Land and Liberty!" Bark paintings of flowers and brilliantly plumed birds decorated a third wall. The paintings surrounded a rubbing of ancient Mayan glyphs and a rendering of a fierce Mayan warrior with a spear, multicolored shield, and feathered headdress.

"This is my daughter Agrafina and my almost-daughter Linda," the general said and gestured to the two young women. "But then you know Linda, don't you, Señor Carter?" The general slapped his thigh and laughed with delight. "The world is very small after all!"

They sat in simple, leather-covered chairs. With the rough wooden tables, handmade furniture, wall decorations, and electric lights, it was the room of a contemporary warrior whose heart was still in the past.

"Tea!" the general commanded, and the two women rose and left. "You will stay with us a few days," the general said, directing his attention to Carter and Tice. "We have a fiesta that starts tonight and runs through tomorrow. You must stay to see that. And your clothes . . ." He gestured disdainfully at the muddy ponchos and camouflage pants Carter and Tice wore. "It will take some time for them to be properly laundered and prepared for you. Meanwhile . . . ah, here is the tea!"

Agrafina carried a tray of steaming pottery mugs, followed by Linda with another tray holding a pitcher and two bowls. They set the trays on a low table in front of the general.

"Honey and milk?" Agrafina asked the two *norteamericanos*, her eyes modestly lowered.

"This is Mayan herbal tea," Linda explained. "Delicious plain."

Carter and Tice took their tea straight, looking at one another as they drank. The general poured honey and milk into his. The women stood behind General Hiler's chair, waiting to serve him.

"Linda," Carter said, "your last name wouldn't happen to be Piedra?"

Linda's eyes went wide with surprise, and the general chuckled.

"I'd heard that Alicia Piedra had a daughter," Carter went on, and he smiled too.

"Alicia!" The general heaved a sigh. "Such a woman!"

"My name is Stone," Linda said, her fingers moving across the back of the general's tall chair. "My mother took the name Piedra when we moved from Houston and she started acting in Mexico City. I was a little girl then."

"Now it makes sense," Carter mused. "The slight Texas accent. Piedra means Stone in Spanish. Your people are originally from England, not Germany. But close enough. Saxons and Vikings, the English."

Linda nodded.

"She grew up with my Agrafina," the general explained,

patting Linda's hand. "She spent summers here at the ranch. Her scarlet mother remarried a few years ago." He smiled to take the sting from his words. The wound had healed, but it still pained him.

Tice had been watching the play between Carter and Linda with interest. He turned to the general.

"I like your ranch," Tice said. "Reminds me of one I grew up on in California."

"Ah! California! That is a different story," the general said and drank some tea. "Our people wade the Rio Grande into Texas and cut the barbed wire into California. There aren't enough jobs and land for them in Mexico. It is a tragedy of evil proportions."

"The people here at Monte Vista seem busy enough," Tice said.

The general shrugged.

"One bean in the chili pot. Not enough to ease the pangs of the multitudes of hungry, or the dreams of the landless. We are an agrarian country, but the postage-stamp farms go to the eldest son, and the younger children are left with nothing but dreams. Most of the land is still controlled by great corporations or ranches."

"Like yours," Carter pointed out.

"No!" The general shook his head emphatically. "Monte Vista is an *ejido* now!"

"Community owned," Carter mused. "But that only complicates the problem. A family can occupy its little piece forever, but it can't sell, rent, or mortgage it. The younger children will still grow up to be landless."

"The sun sets slowly over Monte Vista," the general argued. "There is more than enough land for generations."

"And what about your sons?" Tice wanted to know.

"I have no sons," the general said. "Agrafina will get the hacienda, the land around it, and some land behind the east mountain."

"I will be comfortable," Agrafina said softly, gazing shyly at Tice.

She was in her mid-twenties, a spinster in a land where most Indian girls married at fifteen. Something had prevented her marriage.

Tice grinned at her and ran a hand through his sandy hair.

"She'll be fine," Linda said. "She's much loved here."

The general watched Agrafina and Tice. He frowned.

"I've been admiring your Tree of Life, General," Carter said. "Did you get it in Tuxtla?"

The general turned and gazed at the brightly colored clay and wire creation on the wall. Then his eyes moved to the wall that contained the rubbing of the ancient Mayan carvings.

"Tuxtla Gutiérrez, yes," he said.

"And the serpent is Kukulcán," Carter went on.

"A great god. A Mayan god! And in that tree," the General said and waved at the wall, "it is the center of a Christian story. And why not? We are Mayans first. Thousands of years ago we were a jungle tribe, as innocent and unsophisticated as a monkey in a tree. Yet we grew to build stone cities so magnificent that the first conquistadores thought they were the work of Romans or Phoenicians. There were three million of us! Our cities towered above the jungle!" the general said. Energy radiated from him in hot waves. "Our people spread throughout southern Mexico, Guatemala, El Salvador, and Honduras! We created beautiful works of art! Poetry! An accurate calendar! Writings to record our lives!"

"Papa," Agrafina said hesitantly, pressing a small hand to his shoulder.

Linda's face was white.

"No!" he said. "They should know! We did not build our great cities with slave labor. We had a sense of community, of togetherness. The cities were built *for* the people *by* the people. We gave our labor and time instead of paying taxes. We honored our gods and our people with cities that touched the stars! We were glorious then. For almost four thousand years we were one! Then came the terrible Spanish. Still, the

Maya were the last to fall because we were the most noble fighters. It was the Spaniards' chicken pox and guns that killed us! We did not have a chance!''

"Papa, please," Agrafina said in her soft voice.

The general looked around the room, his black eyes blazing. He lifted a tense hand to pat Agrafina's fingers that gripped his shoulder.

"Do not worry," he told her. "Those who do not care have no heart!" He looked at Carter and Tice. "Today we have a new chance. New times. New ways. We are today's Maya making a better future, but still we must honor our great past. You see that."

"It won't be easy," Tice said, watching the General and glancing at Agrafina.

"*Life* is not easy!" the general said and slapped the flat of his hands against the arms of his chair. "Enough! I have been a poor host. Our guests are wet and tired. Show them to their rooms. Dinner is at sundown."

TWELVE

Nick Carter and Philip Tice were given adjoining rooms that opened onto the left side of the hacienda's U. The young women pointed out big washtubs full of hot, sudsy water in each room and fresh clothes laid out on the beds. Agrafina left, her eyes lingering on the CIA agent who filled his doorway and watched until she was gone.

"I can't come in," Linda whispered after Tice had closed his door. She looked at the courtyard.

Men tended a smoldering barbeque pit and smoked hand-rolled cigarettes. Women carried out tables, cloths, and pottery. They sent inquisitive glances toward Carter and Linda.

Carter looked down at Linda. She leaned against the doorframe, then moved so close to him that his head filled with her musky scent.

"The general wouldn't like us to be obvious," he said. He ran his thumb across a high cheekbone, then down the smooth outline of her face to her chin.

"Tonight," she said. "I have something to tell you. I'll come tonight."

Her eyes closed. She took a deep breath, then marched back toward the living room. She was learning.

Carter went inside the room and closed the door. He undressed and peeled off the bandages that covered his chest.

The wounds had continued to heal, and there was no sign of infection.

He climbed into the short bathtub, his knees folded against his chest, and stared out the window at the verdant mountains that gave the isolated ranch its name—Mountain View. He bathed slowly, soaking his tired body, and remembered the hot eagerness of Linda in Tuxtla Gutiérrez.

Outside, hooves thundered across the hard soil. Cattle lowed. People worked, their shouted conversations full of excitement at the coming fiesta night. Carter watched the sun set, watched vermillion and chartreuse stream across the sky. He watched the day die and knew that he waited for the explosion of violence that bubbled beneath the ordinariness of Rancho Monte Vista.

The door thudded with a knock.

"Come in, Tice," Carter called from the tub.

The big man walked in, dressed in the simple white cotton trousers and shirt of the *campesino*. The sleeves stopped at his forearms, and the trousers ended well above his ankles. He laughed and shrugged beneath the too-tight shirt.

"Not exactly designer fashions," Tice commented.

"You'll never pass," Carter said and laughed.

Tice sat on the cot.

"What do you think?" the CIA man said, suddenly serious.

"I still don't know. The general's excitable. The daughter's worried."

"Some girl, that Agrafina!" Tice said, his blue eyes dancing.

"Stay away from her, Phil. Unless you want to wind up dead."

"I got that impression too."

Carter stood up in the tub, and Tice threw him a towel.

"I like this place," Tice said.

"I know. Agrafina knows, too. And so does the general."

Philip Tice dropped his head into his hands.

"I've been at the work too long, I guess." He shook his

head and looked up. "Too many countries. Last time I was home was in '82. Half the time I'm never sure whether I'm doing any good."

"It's that way for all of us," Carter said, dressing in the rough cotton clothes. "Every once in a while, though, we get a chance to do something we're sure of. Maybe that'll be the way it is this time."

Tice stood and stretched carefully in the tight clothes, an elephant with the grace of a tiger. He reassembled his face into a mask that hid his emotions and showed the world a professional.

"Ready?" Carter asked.

They walked along the porch toward the central living room. Carter carried his briefcase, and Tice his rifle and bandoliers. The courtyard was bright with paper lanterns and Indians dressed in colorful cotton clothes. Three guitarists and a drummer started to play, and the crowd froze then swirled into a fast dance of celebration. The haunting music followed Carter and Tice into the living room.

As they entered, a slight man with Slavic features, dressed in loose peasant clothes, looked up from talking with the general. The man nodded briskly, stood, and left. He brushed past Carter and Tice as if he didn't see them.

"Barkov!" Carter whispered to Tice.

Tice nodded, eyes narrowed.

They watched the KGB's Mexican chief mingle with *campesinos, charros,* and soldiers around the outdoor barbeque pit.

"Sorry I didn't introduce you," the general said, walking toward them with a glass in his hand. "And old friend from Mexico City. Just dropped in this afternoon. Has to leave now."

"Must have flown in," Carter said. "But I didn't hear a plane."

Carter watched Barkov take a plate full of food. Even the KGB has to eat.

"The landing field is over on Agrafina's land," the general said easily. "Behind the east mountain." He waved a glass containing an amber liquid. "May I offer you some aguardiente?"

The homemade sugar cane liquor burned Carter's throat and sent a pleasant glow through him. The general led the two agents onto the outside terra-cotta steps. Laughing and talking, the Indians in the courtyard gathered in front of them, drawn by the general's presence. Still by the barbeque, Barkov ate and watched. His sharp eyes darted around the courtyard as if he owned every arch and tile.

"A healthy life for our general!" a man called.

"A long life! We will prosper together!"

"To Hilario Hiler! One of us!"

The Indians raised bowls and cups in salute. General Hiler had made life good for them, and their gratitude showed in the love on their beaming faces. Hiler returned their smiles.

The general opened his arms.

"Eat! Drink!" His voice rang out across the crowd. "We Maya will show the world a better way to live!"

They gave a shout, then drank from their cups and bowls. The general nodded, smiling, then led Carter and Tice through the throng toward the barbeque. Barkov handed his empty plate to an old woman and moved off, skirting the crowd.

Tice looked questioningly at Carter. Carter nodded, and the CIA man followed the KGB chief.

Linda and Agrafina passed full plates to Carter and the general. Then Agrafina turned to scan the *fiesteros* who merrily ate and danced beneath the stars. From her eager stance, Carter knew she was looking for Tice, but Barkov—with Tice tailing—had left the courtyard and disappeared into the night.

Linda stood next to Carter, eating from her own plate of roasted beef, tortillas, rice, and beans.

"I'm lucky I came here," she said. "I didn't know where else to go . . . after those men took you away. I thought maybe Papa Hiler could help me."

"His men found Tice and me."

They were already out looking when I got here."

"Did Barkov call the general and tell him to find me?"

She shrugged, then pulled the sleeve of her loose dress back over her naked shoulder.

"They're old friends, Papa Hiler and Barkov." She stopped and gazed reflectively at Carter. "Because of the Tree of Life . . . you think they're involved in the Itzamná business?"

"Perhaps."

Four men carrying a litter on poles walked into the center of the crowd. On the litter, set in a bed of ferns, was a statue with reptilian features and a body combining parts of a crocodile, lizard, and snake.

"Speak of the devil!"

"Itzamná himself," Carter breathed and looked at her. "How long since you've visited Monte Vista?"

"Too long."

They watched the litter bearers as they walked through the crowd, their heads high and proud. Each wore colored crosses painted above their eyes. A fifth man followed, carrying a crate of squawking sacrificial chickens. The crowd bowed low, and those with similar crosses painted above their eyes sang and followed the statue down the road toward a big ceremonial hut blazing with light.

General Hiler joined Carter and Linda.

"The old religion speaks again," he said, gesturing at the crowd whose eyes followed the god and worshippers toward the hut. "The Maya of Central America will unite. Once more we will rule ourselves to greatness!"

"The odds are against you," Carter said.

"Go! Follow them if you like. See our sincerity!"

"I don't need to." He smiled at the general. "I believe you. Are you counting on Maxim Barkov to make your plans work?"

The general shrugged and took a drink. His wily eyes assessed Carter. For a moment he was again the jungle hero who fought bravely in Korea and Vietnam.

"He helps us," Hiler said at last. "We accept help from all quarters." The seriousness in his face disappeared into a charming grin. "I would like the help of the United States. A great country, it too began like ours—with a revolution! But ours will be a revolution of peace!"

Carter watched the general thoughtfully.

"Where is Tice?" the general asked, turning his head. "No matter. Go! Dance, drink, sing! Tonight and tomorrow we celebrate our good beginning!" He pushed Carter and Linda away.

Linda took Carter's hand. In the other, Carter carried his briefcase.

"Where to?" she asked.

They gave their plates to the women at the barbeque pit and walked among *charros* and *campesinos* watching the festivities. The men smoked, and the sweet smell of marijuana swirled around them.

"What did you want to tell me?" Carter murmured to her in English.

"A small thing, but perhaps it's important," she said. "The man who tied me up—the one in the Hotel Tuxtla— said something I thought might be useful. I'd wanted to tell you when we were in bed tonight." She squeezed his hand. "You understand."

They walked out of the courtyard, two lovers taking an evening stroll. The intimacy that comes after good lovemaking made all secrets more important.

"And that was?"

"He warned me. He said, 'Get out of Chiapas. Stay out of Cobán.' Then he gagged me."

"Cobán's in Guatemala. There's an airport there."

"Who was he?"

"A Cuban guerrilla. They've been tracking Itzamná since before San Antonio. It's got them worried too, whatever it is."

"How did you get away?"

Carter told her as they walked toward the brightly lit ceremonial hut. Low, moaning singing rose from there and spread into the night. To their right, horses in a big corral stood silent and unmoving as statues.

Carter heard a click. He pulled Wilhelmina from beneath his loose peasant shirt.

Feet scuffled on dirt.

"Stay here!" Carter whispered to Linda.

He ran silently, bending low to the ground.

A body thumped to the packed dirt near the corral.

In the light of the half moon, five figures struggled. Horses whinnied and fled across the corral. A very tall figure picked up another soldier and heaved him away.

Carter flung Hugo through the air.

A man fell, blood streaming black on his green uniform. The stiletto hung from his side, embedded in his heart.

"Thanks!" Tice grunted.

Another figure watched, his peasant clothes gleaming a pale blue in the moonlight. Maxim Barkov. His face was lined in cruel delight. He held two rifles, one his own, the other Tice's.

He heard Carter and whipped around. Effortlessly Carter kicked the rifles away and smashed a fist into Barkov's jaw. The punch was not hard enough to break anything, just hard enough to knock him out. Carter wanted to talk to Barkov.

Tice picked up two soldiers and crashed their faces together. The hollow sound of noses smashing reverberated in the night.

There was a noise of running feet approaching.

Carter retrieved Hugo and kicked the legs out from under the last soldier, a short man who cried out in pain.

As the man fell, he shoved a long knife into Philip Tice's stomach.

Blood gushed.

The big man staggered.

"Nick!" he gasped, pitching over onto his side.

Carter dropped beside him. Tice's hands were wrapped

around the knife. Blood covered his fingers. His face was contorted in pain.

"Don't pull it out!" Carter warned him, then turned.

The new soldiers were on Carter immediately.

Carter jumped up and slashed Hugo across the face of the first. The blood on the stiletto mixed with the cascade streaming from the soldier's face.

Instantly Carter blasted back an elbow into another soldier's rib cage. Bones cracked. The soldier fell, gasping for air.

Carter spun and saw that the odds were still thirty to one.

Carter barreled among four soldiers, knocking them into the corral's fence. They lay draped like scarecrows across the rails, stunned.

"Hold on, Tice!" Carter yelled.

He streaked away.

"Nick!" Linda called out.

Behind him Carter could hear the boots of the soldiers pounding the ground in pursuit.

Linda ran beside him, light and fast as a gazelle.

"This way!" she panted, leading him toward the light and sounds of the ceremonial hut.

Once inside, they slowed, weaving their way among the worshippers.

Across the room, behind an altar, stood Agrafina, resplendent in cape, feathers, and flowers. The altar was low and bowl-shaped. A scarificial altar. The heavy scent of incense hung in the air. The chickens clucked in their cages beside the altar.

The soldiers entered, stirring the dust on the dirt floor as they skidded to slow down.

Carter and Linda threaded their way toward Agrafina, the soldiers behind in slow but steady pursuit. The men smiled grimly. They had cornered Carter.

The worshippers raised dazed faces, bewildered. Agrafina chanted. Her eyes were closed. Her soft voice filled the room with its intensity.

"Agrafina!" Linda cried.

The young woman's eyes snapped open. She glared at the interruption.

"Philip Tice is hurt!" Carter called. "Outside by the corral!"

Carter and Linda reached the altar.

Agrafina frowned, still in another world.

The soldiers closed in, their rifles pointed at Carter.

Agrafina seemed to shake herself, then she saw the soldiers and guns.

"Stop!" Agrafina cried, raising her arms in command.

The soldiers slowed but still moved forward, a circle of impending death.

Carter whirled on them, Wilhelmina in hand. It was a standoff. The soldiers' eyes wavered, but still they advanced. A moan swept through the crowd. Some fled out the door. Others stood frozen. Agrafina stared at the soldiers, her face composed and regal. She refused to leave.

Carter raised the toe of his sandal. He watched the advancing soldiers.

"I command you!" Agrafina shouted. "Stop!"

If Carter fired, the soldiers would, too. They might hit Linda and Agrafina. His trained gaze swept around the room. Behind Agrafina was a tapestry of woven cotton. The plumed serpent Kukulcán was emblazoned in glory on the tapestry next to the statue of Itzamná. Beneath the cloth, Carter's sharp eyes saw the vague outlines of a door.

With the toe of his sandal, Carter unlatched the cage of the sacrificial chickens.

He dropped, tossing the box of chickens high.

Bullets whined past him, thudding into the tapestry.

The chickens screeched into the air. Feathers flew. Wings beat the soldiers' faces. Claws grabbed at them, trying to find a foothold.

"No!" Agrafina cried, reaching for a flapping chicken.

Carter snatched her hand.

"Come on!" he shouted at Linda.

He wrenched up the tapestry and pushed the women outside.

Carter turned, crouched, and fired Wilhelmina into the forehead of the closest soldier.

The angry soldier's claw-ripped face exploded at such close range. He pitched onto the sacrificial altar, filling the bowl with his own blood.

The other soldiers froze.

Carter streaked out the door.

Immediately bullets shot through the tapestry in pursuit.

"Philip!" Agrafina called. She picked up her skirts and ran toward the horse corral.

Carter and Linda raced toward the hacienda.

"Where to?" Linda shouted.

"Stay here!" Carter commanded.

He put on a burst of speed that left her complaining far behind. She wouldn't be able to catch up, and she'd be safe with Agrafina at Monte Vista.

Carter circled around the hacienda. In the courtyard teeming with people, General Hiler again stood on the broad terra-cotta steps. Disheveled soldiers were reporting to him. The general's face was red with fury.

Carter dashed east and found a wide trail. A soldier was loading crates of supplies onto the back of a jeep.

Silently Carter padded forward.

The soldier worked happily, humming a mariachi tune under his breath. He'd already eaten. The barbeque smell of beef and beans clung to his clothes.

Carter wrapped an arm around the soldier's throat and jerked.

The soldier fell, unconscious, his eyes rolling up into his head. He'd be out for a long time.

Carter pried up a thin plank from one of the supply boxes. Gleaming new AK-47 rifles were neatly packed stock to barrel. Russian rifles, supplied by Barkov. Carter threw the crate into the road, watching with satisfaction as the box burst apart and the rifles tumbled into the jungle.

He stripped the uniform off the limp soldier and put it on. It was short, tight in the shoulders, and loose in the waist, but it would do. Carter climbed into the jeep.

He drove up the rutted mountain road. Every hundred yards he tossed another crate of rifles to smash into the underbrush until the boxes were gone. He chuckled, pleased. Parrots called. Insects buzzed. Leaves fluttered in the growing breeze. The jungle was friendly, and Carter's jeep climbed the difficult road with ease.

From the top of the mountain, he could see the airfield below. It was a mass of shadows, some shadows darker than others. In the moonlight, his penetrating eyes could see that leafy branches had been dragged over the planes so they wouldn't be noticed from the air. There were about two dozen planes. Occasional glimmers of metal shone faintly as the jeep descended toward the valley floor.

A sentry stood slouched against a tree where the road entered Agrafina's property. The tip of the sentry's cigarette glowed orange in the night.

Carter dipped his head so his non-Indian face wouldn't be seen. He waved.

The sentry nodded sleepily and waved in return.

Carter drove on, grinning. He was dressed right and drove an official vehicle. People saw what they expected to see.

As he drove past, he looked closely at the camouflaged planes. There were both U.S. Navy and Russian jets. He wasn't surprised. General Hiler—and Colonel Barkov—had connections that produced.

He circled the airfield and saw occasional clusters of soldiers. Some played cards in the light of flashlights. Others smoked alone, sitting on boulders or leaning against trees.

At last Carter found it: the Westwind he'd left in Tuxtla Gutiérrez. Linda had arrived at Rancho Monte Vista before he had, long before a trip by road would have gotten her there. She'd have had to fly in. Besides being beautiful, she was intelligent and had more skills than she liked to admit. Even to Carter.

Mentally he thanked her and climbed on board. When he turned on the motors, he saw soldiers jerk to attention. They ran toward his turbojet. Their mouths were shaped with shouts he couldn't hear over the roar of the engines.

He taxied onto the takeoff strip. A trail of soldiers fired rifles behind him. Bullets streaked past his windows, and he felt the impact of three bullets in the tail section. He moved the plane faster. As the soldiers fell farther and farther behind, he thought of Philip Tice and hoped he would survive. But there was nothing he could do for the CIA man now. The mission came first—and that would be what Tice wanted.

Carter felt the turbojet's wheels lift off the ground, the first moment of suspension and then of flight. Behind and below, the stick figures of soldiers jumped up and down in frustration. Carter noted the coordinates, then took off into the starry night.

He flew for fifteen minutes, appreciating the plane's steadiness, a reliable old friend now. The jungled mountains rose and fell below in a turbulent black sea. Occasional points of light showed cookfires or jeeps roaming the lonely mountains.

He turned on the radio. It crackled and then was silent as the connections met.

"This is getting to be a habit, N3," Hawk growled from Washington. "You could report in during the day. Anytime you'd like."

"I seem to be tied up days, sir."

"Bit of a joke, N3. Glad to hear from you," Hawk puffed and chuckled in the distance. "Where the hell are you?"

"Leaving General Hilario Hiler's ranch in Chiapas." Carter told Hawk what had happened there. "There were about two dozen U.S. Navy and Soviet planes stored not far away. And a good landing strip."

"Ties up with the jet in New Mexico that picked up Santos."

"I thought you'd think that, sir."

"And now we've got Maxim Barkov on the spot where

there's some action. MI5 assures me they're going to have a report from one of their agents for me soon. Seems there are indications that more than just Mexico is involved in It-zamná.''

''Probably any country that has Mayan Indians,'' Carter said.

There was a pause. Carter imagined Hawk leaning toward his big ashtray.

''That's right, N3,'' Hawk's distant voice rumbled. ''Nothing yet about the Navy, or about who's supplying the Indians from here. But I'll find out.'' Hawk's voice was harsh, then softened. ''You have the coordinates on that ranch?''

Carter gave them to him.

''I trust you're on your way to Cobán now?''

''Right.''

''Be careful, Nick. This seems to be getting bigger.'' Hawk puffed and blew.

''I'll keep that in mind.''

''I know you will,'' Hawk said.

THIRTEEN

The man who walked through the busy Cobán airport wore a secondhand polyester business suit. Nick Carter read the *Wall Street Journal*, leaned against a wall, and watched him. Carter had been there for hours, propping up different walls, and his feet ached from lack of a day's use. He watched the man stand in line at the candy counter, a package wrapped in newspaper and tied with twine at his feet. It was heavy. Every time he took a step forward in line, he pushed the package ahead of him with his feet.

The man bought two chocolate bars and paid for them with a hand on which two fingers were missing. He was one of the Cubans from Tuxtla and the jungle cave with the Mayan wall paintings.

Carter picked up his briefcase and followed the Cuban out the door to a taxi stand where one old Chevrolet waited. The window was open, and the driver's head rested on the car door. He was asleep.

The Cuban got into the back seat. When the door slammed, the driver jerked awake. The Cuban gave him directions that Carter couldn't hear.

The taxi sputtered, and the motor turned over. It drove slowly down the street.

Carter looked at a line of battered cars and trucks. In an old Ford pickup loaded with vegetables, a man sat behind the wheel, a straw hat pulled low over his eyes. It was early afternoon, siesta time, and the warm day made even working people tired.

Carter picked up the sign that listed vegetables and prices and got into the cab of the produce truck.

The driver looked at Carter, sleep still in his eyes. Carter waved a twenty-dollar bill. The driver's eyes focused, widened with surprise, then with pleasure. In Central America, American dollars still talk.

"I don't kill nobody," the driver said in English, his gaze glued to the money.

"You don't have to," Carter said in Spanish and smiled. "Just follow that taxi."

"*Sí, hombre!*" The driver sat up. "I have seen plenty of American movies!"

They drove down cobbled streets lined with houses, then with shacks, traveling northeast toward the mountains.

"You trying to catch this guy?" the driver wanted to know. He opened a pack of Juicyfruit gum and chewed.

"I think I'll let him catch me." Carter winked at the driver. "But I can't be too obvious."

"*Entiendo.*" The driver nodded as if he understood.

He turned on his radio, and they listened to a popular music station as they dropped back to trail the taxi to a small tarpaper shack on the outskirts of town.

"We'll wait here," Carter told the driver.

They parked, the rough engine idling.

The Cuban paid off his taxi driver and sent him away. His eyes scanned the area, looked briefly at the vegetable truck, then moved on to check workers carrying loads, women strolling with children who tugged at their skirts, and a young man leaning over a broken fence to talk to his sweetheart. Daily life was the same in all countries.

The Cuban went into the shack and came out five minutes later. He still carried the package, but now he was dressed in his mottled green and brown guerrilla clothes.

The Cuban got into a jeep and continued on the road that led into the mountains.

"Let's go!" Carter's driver said enthusiastically. He jerked the pickup into gear.

"You like movies?" Carter asked him as they followed on the dusty road.

"Ah, *The French Connection!*" the driver said. "Now *that* was some car chase! And James Bond? *Muy heroico!*"

"Very much a hero," Carter agreed. "Unfortunately, agents in real life don't solve problems quite so easily," he added under his breath in English.

"Qué dice?" asked the driver.

Carter translated, and the driver nodded thoughtfully.

"Me, I always wanted to be a hero," the driver said.

"Selling vegetables is important too."

"Someday I will show them!" the driver went on. "Someday I will be a real hero!" He raised a fist and waved it like a flag.

The afternoon stretched into the constant drone of the pickup's engine, the dust that clogged their throats and covered their clothes, and the green walls that grew up around them as they entered the lush jungle.

When the sun was low over the treetops, the Cuban's jeep put on a sudden burst of speed and disappeared around a bend.

"You'd better let me out here," Carter said. The driver was obviously disappointed. "It'd be safer for you."

The driver narrowed his eyes.

"What are you going to do?" the driver asked.

"It's better you don't know," Carter said. "I'll get out here."

"No!"

The driver pressed the accelerator to the floor, and the old pickup lurched forward. The tall jungle trees closed over the top of the road. They were riding in a green tunnel.

They drove around the bend.

Bullets shot past them, exploding two tires.

Carter pulled out Wilhelmina and his billfold.

The driver stared in shock at the Luger.

The pickup weaved, then wobbled to a stop.

Guerrillas dropped from the trees onto the pickup's hood and the bed behind.

The driver whirled around.

"My vegetables!" he cried.

Carter handed him forty dollars.

"Sorry about that," he said and jumped out.

The driver clambered onto the road. He ran around the pickup, staring at the two ruined tires. He held his head and moaned at the guerrillas tromping across his produce.

"Bastards!" he yelled and waved his fists. "You are killing my vegetables!"

"I will take that," the Cuban with two fingers missing told Carter as he picked up Carter's briefcase.

"I thought you might," Carter said. "Think you can help him with his tires?"

The Cuban frowned, then directed a man over to the irate driver.

The driver swung a fist, but the guerrilla caught it and spoke softly to the vegetable man. Together they stared sorrowfully at the flat tires.

"Thanks for the lift!" Carter called to the distracted driver. He turned to the guerrilla who held his briefcase. "Who's in charge?"

The man in charge was a Nicaraguan woman with jet black hair and ebony eyes. Felicia Santos was her name. Her guerrilla shirt was pulled tightly across high breasts, and her pants hugged womanly hips, then bagged down to her feet.

"Any relation to Tiger Santos?" Carter asked as he accepted a cup of hot coffee. He held it but didn't drink.

They sat on a fallen log in the guerrilla camp that overlooked an uninhabited valley. Behind them stood the tall Cuban leader from Tuxtla Gutiérrez. He stood at ease, a watchful second-in-command.

The Cubans' camp was tidy, compact, and designed for secrecy. The road to it was hidden at the intersection with the main road by branches and brush pulled across every time a vehicle entered. The guerrillas used stoves that gave off no smoke, and their tents were the color of the trees that arched overhead.

"Don't worry," she laughed. "We value our coffee too much to put anything into it." She watched him and drank from her own cup. "My brother—Tiger—loves coffee."

"And murder," Carter said and drank.

Felicia Santos sighed.

"*Sí*, I'm afraid that is so. When did you meet him?"

"I haven't yet. But I followed his trail once."

"Recently," she said. "We only kicked him out three months ago."

"This week," he said. "Ended up in Chiapas."

She nodded and drank deeply.

Around them, guerrillas were dismantling tents, packing supplies, readying to leave.

"José!" she called to the guerrilla missing two fingers. "Pack the new radio carefully!"

José rewrapped the radio in the newspaper and twine he'd had in Cobán. It was the same radio that he'd used to alert the guerrillas that Nick Carter was tailing him.

"My brother is the baby of the family," Felicia said. "My father called him *tigre* to make him fierce, a man. The older he grew, the less of a man he was—more like a wild animal."

"Names influence us," Carter said, "for good or bad."

She nodded, and her loose hair fell across her face.

"Does my brother have anything to do with Itzamná?"

"It appears so. But I don't know the extent of his connection."

"Has your country been losing materiel? Money?" she asked.

Carter studied her. She was in her late twenties and had risen to her position of responsibility through seasoning. Her face showed the strain of her work in the flatness of the skin, taut with years of tension and sun, and the way her eyes constantly worked the scene around her. She missed nothing.

"Maybe," Carter replied. "Why?"

She studied him in return. Her gaze flickered over him, digesting the muscled physique and the handsome, intelligent face. She lingered over Wilhelmina resting on his knee. Not arguing whether he could keep the Luger was another gesture from the band, this one an invitation.

Her gaze returned to his face and, for just a moment, he saw lust in her luminous eyes. Quickly she veiled them.

"There is someone you must meet," she decided. "Someone who must meet you. You will come with us."

"What if I don't want to come?"

"It is about Itzamná," she said and laughed knowingly. "You will come."

Carter, Felicia Santos, and all but two of the guerrillas loaded pickups and jeeps, and drove the dusty road around and down the Guatemalan mountain. The two men left behind would maintain the camp for any Marxist group that needed it.

Night fell rapidly as they drove. Jungle sounds decreased as nocturnal predators came out to hunt. The vehicles entered the sleeping city of Cobán close to midnight and drove directly to the airport.

"We have an arrangement," Felicia said to Carter's questioning look. "Sympathizers let us use the landing field and protect us."

They drove around the main building to an area where small planes were stored. Carter's turbojet was gone. He stared at the place where he'd left it secured. Thieves . . . or Linda again? Carter wondered.

The group flew south in a light transport. The back was crowded with guerrillas sitting in seats and in the aisle. Carter rode in front with the pilot: Felicia. She manned the controls as if she were part of the machine, her hair back over her shoulders, her face always looking eagerly into the night.

"Managua?" Carter asked.

"Of course," she replied. "Where I was born."

"Yet you fight with a Cuban band in Guatemala."

"We are one. We fight for freedom and land. It is the same cause whatever the country."

The night was as clear and shiny as wet ink. The stars sparkled. The half moon was encased in a silver halo. Felicia's intensity suited the night's beauty, reflected back on it as an endless lake does the sky.

"Managua struggles for a better life," she went on, "with little help from the United States. Your country has put on so much pressure that we cannot get the bank loans we need." She took her gaze from the night to look accusingly at Carter.

"A political decision," he said. "Besides, we've been lending you money for years. We've kept Nicaragua from going bankrupt."

"Nevertheless," she said and returned her eyes to the controls, "it hurts our people. In the women's hospital, there aren't enough supplies. Premature babies are stuffed two and three to an incubator. New mothers can stay in the hospital only one day because there is not enough clean linen. And the washers and dryers—like most medical machines—are made in the United States. They cost tens of thousands of dollars to repair. Our government does not have the cash."

"There's never enough money," Carter said. "Anywhere."

She shook her head and the black hair flew.

"Excuses!" she accused. "Nothing but excuses while people suffer and die!"

"I don't like people to suffer any more than you do," Carter said. "But governments can only give so much foreign aid. Even the United States has to have limits."

She pursed her lips and was silent. It was an unresolvable issue, and she knew it. Still, she would fight on.

As dawn turned the horizon gray and rose, the group landed at Managua's airport. They walked past sleepy passengers and vendors to the front of the building. Street hawkers urged them to buy pottery, cloth, and vegetables.

"*Huevos, señor?*" said a crippled old peasant dressed in rags. He scuttled toward Carter, eggs in a box before him. He held two eggs high, passing them beneath the noses of the guerrillas as he approached the *norteamericano* who looked as if he might have some money. "*Huevos frescos!*" he called. He had a drooping white cavalryman's mustache. His shoulders were hunched as if numerous bones had been broken and healed incorrectly. He looked directly up into Carter's eyes. "The freshest!" he crowed in Spanish, then whispered, "Wouldn't happen to have a burner, would you, Nicky, old boy?"

Carter grinned as Cecil Young, MI5 from British Intelligence, supposedly retired, sailed on, looking for more receptive buyers. Carter didn't turn around. He continued with the guerrillas who, once at the curb, piled into dusty limousines that creaked and sputtered. Then they all drove into the city.

The limousine in which Carter and Felicia rode stopped before an impressive mansion near the heart of town. It was marked with neglect. Weeds choked the front garden, tiles were cracked on the low wall that surrounded it, and someone had abandoned an old overstuffed armchair on the sidewalk in front.

Carter and Felicia walked up to the massive front doors.

"The bell does not work," Felicia explained and opened a door.

"Carlos!" she called. "Are you up?"

Carter, Felicia, and Colonel Carlos Ek breakfasted in a vast, cavernous room that had once been majestic. Half-dead greenery struggled for survival against pearl white walls. An indoor reflecting pool was rimmed with algae and dirty gray mineral deposits from the evaporating water. The furniture was shoved to one end of the room, while at the other end, beyond the pool, wooden storage crates were stacked. The crates were stamped with the Spanish words for ammo and rations.

The colonel pushed a button, and the ceiling rippled back in accordian pleats to display a bright morning sky. There were no windows in the room.

"I've only been here a year," Colonel Ek explained and sat at the glass-topped table. "The man who owned it moved to Switzerland—a Nicaraguan capitalist who made his money in wheat, cotton gins, and vegetable oils." The colonel chuckled and lifted a cup of hot chocolate. "He didn't get to take much with him, except his life."

"Since the Revolution," Felicia said, "our people have housing, medical care, and many more schools. Health care and education are basic rights. Two years before the Revolution—in 1977—there were nineteen thousand doctor visits. Last year there were six million. It is progress, and the Revolution moves forward!"

"What about the continued fighting and deaths?" Carter asked. "Is that progress too?"

Colonel Ek stood, hitched up his pants, and strode around the room. He was slender and restless, and had the stooped shoulders of a man who grew up reading books.

"It is the contras!" he said. "The counterrevolutionaries who make progress difficult! Your country finances them, and they swarm out of Honduras and assassinate our teachers and professionals. If you won't help us, at least leave us alone! Nicaragua's model government can be repeated in all countries in Central and South America. The United States does not want this. It wants to keep us in subjugation!"

Carter sighed. The hot eggs and toast before him cooled.

"In war, there's right and wrong on both sides," he said quietly. "You know that yourselves. Marxist principles look good on paper maybe, but when put into action, they take away a person's basic freedom to achieve. Personal fulfillment is important too."

The colonel slouched back into his cedar chair. He lifted his fork and eyed Carter speculatively.

"So! We agree to disagree?" He smiled suddenly as if beliefs like everything else were terminal. The pleasure of the moment had its own value. He ate.

Voices floated into the vast room from the rest of the mansion. Doors opened and closed. The house was alive with laughter and business talk. A soldier in a sharp uniform walked into the room and paused just inside the doorway. He carried a sheaf of papers and a pen. Colonel Ek waved his arm.

"Come in, Ricardo. I will look at them."

As Colonel Ek scanned the pages and signed his name, Felicia Santos touched Carter's arm.

"I'm hungry, aren't you?" she said.

They ate, the food still warm and aromatic. New energy poured through Carter. It had been a long week.

When the soldier left, Colonel Ek returned to his breakfast.

"I understand you've also been losing money and materiel," Carter said.

"What?" Colonel Ek looked at him sharply, then frowned at Felicia.

"I did not tell him," she said and shrugged.

"A simple deduction," Carter said. "Do you know yet who's funneling off the cash and equipment?"

Colonel Ek shook his head, worried.

"We are not sure."

"Could it be Maxim Barkov?" Carter asked.

The Nicaraguan colonel chewed thoughtfully.

"It is a good possibility," he said. "But why would he?"

"Itzamná," Carter said.

"That again!" the colonel exploded. "What in hell is Itzamná?"

"I'm not sure yet," Carter said, "but Barkov is definitely involved."

"Who else?" Felicia asked.

"Your brother Tiger, and possibly the Indians."

"It is said in my family that we have a Mayan past," the colonel said. "Ek is a Mayan name—it means stars. The family's history is cloudy, but Indian blood runs in most Central Americans' veins. But the Maya are an impoverished people. They have no power. What could they be up to?"

"Maybe nothing themselves," Carter said.

"Do you have a radio?" Colonel Ek asked, finishing his breakfast.

"In my briefcase."

"You will keep us posted. What little money we have must go to our causes. We do not want it to go to works of evil."

Carter smiled.

"No one wants that."

The colonel stood up again.

"I have to get back. The papers pile up. You both must be tired, having been up all night." He shook Carter's hand. "I will see you again later. Tonight for dinner. Stay in the house until we have time to finish our talk and make some agreements."

"Is that an order?" Carter asked with a grin.

Felicia Santos laughed.

"Of course!" she said. "But I will take good care of you."

"Remember," Colonel Carlos Ek said as he walked toward the door, "we have no wish to harm you. Much better that you carry our message back to Washington."

Felicia tossed her mane of ebony hair.

They picked up their dishes and carried them out the door and along a hall full of light. Large glass doors opened at the end onto a tangled garden. Before they reached the doors, Carter and Felicia turned right into a kitchen where men and women soldiers and civilians stood around a coffee urn, talking.

"Felicia! It has been a long time!" a woman said and wrapped her arms around the guerrilla leader.

They hugged, then Felicia Santos introduced Carter to the group.

Soon Felicia led Carter through rooms teeming with more people. She pointed out paintings abandoned by the millionaire owner. Picasso, Monet, and Manet. None by Nicaraguan artists. She showed him Oriental rugs, marble statues, and empty fountains carved with nudes and cupids. Then she took him up the stairs.

Her body's curves swayed gracefully. She was an independent woman, the new Latin woman with a mind of her own. The distant aroma and gleam of the jungle clung to her, a lush tropical plant brought indoors for a short visit.

File cabinets and rough shelves with binders full of official records lined the upstairs hall. Some of the bedroom doors were open. Inside, typewriters clattered and telephones rang.

The guerrilla leader took the AXE Killmaster into a spacious bedroom whose walls were decorated with Nicaraguan art: watercolors of workers in fields; a photograph of Lake Managua with the sun setting hot and orange on the horizon; and a line drawing of a mountain clearing where coffee plants grew toward harvest.

"This is Colonel Ek's room," Carter guessed.

Felicia nodded and walked to the large four-poster bed. The sky-blue chenille coverlet had been pulled neatly across the bed. She touched fringe that covered a pillow.

"Close the door," she said quietly. She looked up, her eyes dark and hungry.

Carter kicked the door closed. The room was silent. They were alone.

He walked to her and smiled.

"I would like to nap," she murmured, "wouldn't you?"

She unbuttoned his shirt and ran her hands up and over his chest, eager hands that were hot against his skin.

"You're not tired," he said and pulled her toward him. Her head fell back, laughing.

She tasted of salt and fresh grass. Her tan throat throbbed beneath his lips.

"No, I'm not tired," she confessed.

He picked her up and buried his face in her breasts. She smelled of sun and mountain streams.

He placed her onto the bed.

Felicia sat up, and slowly unbuckled his belt and unzipped his trousers. Her lips circled his navel, then her tongue traced little patterns on its way down his belly. Silken hair brushed the tops of his thighs as her hands pushed his trousers all the way down his legs.

Carter let the heat from her mouth engulf him until he could wait no longer.

He pushed her back onto the bed and stripped off her blouse, shoes, and pants. She wore no underwear. Felicia lay passive, eyes flashing. She was a Modigliani nude, all curves, planes, and steaming sensuality.

"I want you," she growled. "Now!"

She pulled him down on top of her and swallowed him into her. The room became their own universe, an infinity filled with her cries.

A tapping at the window awoke Carter. A light tapping, rhythmic as raindrops, but there was no storm outside in the dusk. Instead, grinning at him through the glass was Cecil Young, the septuagenarian British agent Carter had worked with on a case not long ago.

Carter nodded and smiled, then gently picked up Felicia Santos's arm from across his chest and moved it to her side. She murmured and curled into a ball, a serene smile on her sleeping face.

Carter went to the window and eased it open.

"Good work, Nicky!" Cecil Young whispered. "You do have a way with the ladies!"

"It's about time," Carter countered, then grinned. "It's good to see you. What took you so long?"

The old gentleman climbed in briskly, and they shook hands.

"Reconnaissance work, old boy. I'm on the Itzamná business that our pencil pushers have been talking to your pencil pushers about. Great good fortune that I ran into you at the airport. Last time I heard, you were in Chiapas."

"Two days ago. It seems a lot longer."

Carter leaned out the window. An immense ivy vine trailed up the side of the mansion, as wild and untended as the gardens. Its leaves were broken where Cecil Young had climbed. Soldiers stood below, unaware of the intruder as they smoked and chatted.

"The silly blighters guard only the grounds," Young explained softly and jovially in his clipped Oxbridge accent. "Never bothered to look up once. Jolly good luck, eh?"

"With you it's never luck, Cecil," Carter said with respect as he dressed. "You watched them first, knew what they'd do."

Young clapped the Killmaster lightly on the shoulder.

He'd lived to a ripe, productive old age in a profession so dangerous that life insurance was a joke.

"You're an astute lad," the old gentleman said.

In the bed across the room, Felicia Santos murmured in her sleep. She tossed covers away to expose round, pendulous breasts.

Young padded to the bed and stared down approvingly. As he smoothed his thick white mustache, brown makeup came off on his fingers and revealed the pink English skin on his face.

"Now what have we here? This is certainly some guerrilla leader, eh?" he whispered. "Wasn't too hard to figure what would happen when I saw you two. And not too hard to find out where you were going. Which bedroom was another matter!" The British agent launched into his story in flawless Spanish, unstoppable in his enthusiasm. " 'But *señora*,' " he quietly mimicked himself and straightened his vender's rags, " 'Señorita Santos ordered the rolls and pastries herself! The best cakes in all Managua! Shall I call up to her window? She will be angry to miss them!' The *señora* in the kitchen is shocked. She glances up, a reflex action, and I know which corner of the mansion you're in! So I hand her the cakes to give to Señorita Santos when she awakens, and stroll down the sidewalk until it's safe to make a dash in." He lifted his hands. "*Voilà!* I'm here!" He spun around, and his rags flared out like birds' wings.

"You are amazing, Cecil," Carter said with amusement.

Felicia Santos sat bolt upright, her eyes wide with surprise. She looked frantically around the bed for her belt and the gun that it held.

Carter kicked it across the room.

"Sorry, Felicia," he said, "I've got to leave."

She ran toward the door, but Carter caught her around the middle. She kicked and screamed. He wrapped a hand over her mouth. She bit him.

"Damn!"

He clapped the hand again over her mouth and carried her

struggling to the bed while Cecil Young held his sides and laughed.

"If it's not too much trouble, Cecil?"

The old agent swallowed and took off his frayed shirt, which he quickly tore into strips.

"I must say that I have been longing for one of your fine burners, Nicky," the old gentleman suggested. "These Central Americans make burners that taste like horse fodder. If you have some, we might go outside for a quiet smoke."

"Of course, Cecil."

They gagged the furious young woman, and tied her ankles and wrists together, then tied them to the head and foot of the four-poster.

"I've had a delightful time, Felicia," Carter said politely as he worked. "And I thank you very much. Perhaps next time we'll meet under better circumstances."

Finished, the men stood back. Cecil Young stared thoughtfully at the naked woman. Her breasts heaved as she pulled against the restraints.

"I suppose it would be decent to cover her," he said.

"Yes. I suppose it would."

"You or I?" Cecil Young said.

"Your choice, sir."

"It is a pity."

With regret, the old agent threw the chenille coverlet across the young woman.

"Perhaps next time we'll have a formal introduction," he told her and smiled.

She opened her mouth wide but only a furious, frustrated grunt escaped. She yanked against the bindings, and her eyes blazed with death promises.

"Careful you don't swallow that gag," Cecil Young advised.

He and Carter sauntered to the window.

"May I give you a lift, sir?" Carter asked.

"Delighted," the old gentleman said. He looked out and down, then climbed through the window.

FOURTEEN

Nick Carter flagged a taxi that took him and Cecil Young to the Managua airport. Young had his first cigarette in the back seat of the taxi, and his second in the pilot's seat of an old, twin-engine British plane that coughed and wheezed as it reluctantly let go of land to glide into flight.

"I think Villahermosa is logical, lad. What do you say?"

"An excellent choice. "I'm known in Tuxtla Gutiérrez."

Now airborne and flying north, the old craft purred. Young adjusted the controls and sat back to smoke.

"It's good to see you, my boy. The damnedest things are happening around here."

"Apparently," Carter said and lit a cigarette for himself.

Cecil Young inhaled deeply and blew out three perfect smoke rings. From experience, Carter knew the old agent couldn't be hurried. He watched as Young wiped a rag across his face and rubbed off the brown makeup.

"Bloody awful stuff," Young said gaily as he stared at the muddy rag. "Invented for actors, but then we're all actors in our own way. Especially in our line of work right, lad?"

Carter nodded and smoked.

"Perhaps you'd like to hear what I've learned," Carter said. He hoped it might get Young started. He told the old agent the story as they flew through the night sky toward Mexico.

"A bit of a sticky wicket, eh?" the old agent murmured and blew more smoke rings. "But I do love a good mystery, and this certainly seems to be adding up to one. I remember the time Teddy—he's the Saudi PM, remember?"

"One of the king's brothers," Carter said, smiling.

"You do have a good memory, lad," Cecil said, warming to his tale. "I remember the time Teddy lost his favorite polo pony. What a fuss! Those Saudis do have bad tempers when little things go wrong. Great in a disaster, but let the soap on the sink be the wrong brand, and everyone from servants to wives is threatened with mutilation."

"Part of their culture," Carter said.

"Exactly! So Teddy called me in and laid out the problem. I went through the stables, talked to his multitudinous children and all the grooms and trainers. Do you know what I found when I finally tracked it down? The horse had been shipped to the United States as a present for the President! A mistake of ridiculous proportions! Poor Teddy couldn't do a thing. A day later he got a handwritten thank-you note on White House stationery from the First Lady. That was the final straw. Teddy fired the trainer who'd been responsible and went on a drinking binge. He surfaced in Morocco two weeks later with a terrible hangover, the trainer in tow, and a new stallion to work up for polo. Teddy paid five hundred thousand U.S. dollars for it!" Cecil Young grinned wickedly at Carter. "Bet you can't guess where the horse came from!"

"California?" Carter said and watched the British agent as he jounced with glee on his seat.

"Yes! The President's ranch! Teddy paid a bloody fortune to get even!"

They laughed, and the old agent wiped teary eyes with the rag.

"Oh, dear God!" Young chortled on. "Money means nothing to the rich! That polo pony has turned out to be the best Teddy has, and now he's vindicated!"

They laughed again at the stubbornness of human pride as the plane sped north under the starry sky.

"Which brings me to my point," the old gentleman said at last.

"And that is?"

"Why, the United States Navy, of course! It follows as night follows day. Your President isn't going to let the Central Americans step ahead in line. Think of Beirut! Lebanon's like Teddy's original polo pony. The President knows no one's really going to win there. And he's going to make bloody damned sure the same doesn't happen here. This is a new stallion that he's got a fair chance at."

"The President . . . he must have done something since I talked to Hawk last night," Carter said.

"Precisely! And this is big, lad. Hold onto your ears. Sometime this morning he sent a half-dozen ships from the fleet to sit off Nicaragua!"

"That's enough firepower to blast away a quarter of Nicaragua's population!"

Young nodded solemnly.

"They're still in international waters. The big gumshoes sit out there with their automated cannons," Young said and waved an arm east, "while the whole Nicaraguan navy consists of two old yachts with one gun each."

"It's a show of strength," Carter mused. "Reminds them of our interest. That whatever Itzamná is, we won't allow it to spread into major war throughout Central America. The Monroe Doctrine."

"Right, lad. The Russian and U.S. Navy jets you told me about at the Hiler ranch must have persuaded him that something needed to be done instantly. He doesn't want an invasion like the Cubans tried to pull in Grenada. But he can't just go in and blast them all away either."

"We have to find another way for him," Carter said.

Cecil Young nodded reflectively, and they sat back to smoke and think.

Near Villahermosa, the small craft flew over the Reforma oil fields that surrounded the large Mexican city. The fields sparkled with red and white lights as the oil rigs pumped black gold into Mexico's ailing economy. In 1938 the government had paid American and British oil companies $129 billion in exchange for control of a resource so rich it is now estimated to be twelve times the reserves of Alaska's North Slope. The gamble had paid off for Mexico.

Nick Carter considered this as they circled over Villahermosa's airport. Whatever the country, to stay in power governments had to provide their people with the necessities of life. If they didn't, a new election—or war—would unseat them.

"Your burners are a delightful treat, Nicky. You're a good lad to share them with me," Cecil Young said as he put out his last.

"Anytime, Cecil."

"I've been wondering about the general's priestess daughter. Do you think she knows what's going on?"

The plane circled and dropped its landing gear.

"I'm not even convinced the general does," Carter said. "As for Agrafina"—he shrugged—"I think her interest has been focused only on her father and her religion for years."

"Nasty business, that. A father shouldn't keep a girl from marrying. A healthy sex life ensures longevity!" Cecil Young winked and grinned.

"So *that's* your secret," Carter said. "And all along I thought you were just a good agent!"

"Follow my advice, Nicky, and you'll live not only long, but well!" The seventy-three-year-old agent roared with laughter.

The plane slowed, weaving between two plumes of orange-yellow fire that streaked into the night sky. Along with the massive oil deposits came discoveries of immense fields of natural gas. The waste gas would burn for days, turning the night into day.

"We're here, lad. At last! And on to new adventure!"

Cecil Young chortled as the plane touched the landing strip.

• • •

At midmorning, Carter and Cecil Young abandoned their jeep in the shadowy jungle at the side of a road that led toward Rancho Monte Vista. They sat under a cedar tree covered with moss and had one last cigarette.

"It's times like this I miss the desert," Young said and picked a tick from his hand.

"Will you go back to Saudi Arabia when you're finished here?" Carter asked.

"Wore out my welcome there, I'm afraid, lad. They know I'm an agent now, so it's on to greener pastures or, in this case, jungles."

They smoked and watched clouds float languidly in the deep blue sky far above the treetops. There is a moment before the beginning of action—before a track race, before a football game, before a soldier goes into battle—that is full of peace and contentment. The moment is preceded and followed by nerves and doubts, but in that single lull the runner, the football player, and the soldier know irrevocably that what they are doing is right. Nick Carter thought about this as he and Cecil Young stood, both full of eagerness and resolution. They stared into the jungle where they would find the answers to their questions.

"We'll separate here," Carter said.

"Cover more territory that way," the old agent agreed. His eyes hungrily scanned the vegetation. "We've got our machetes and compasses."

"The jeep can't be traced."

The two professionals ground their cigarettes into the moist duff and shook hands. They heaved backpacks over their shoulders. Carter picked up the cigarette butts and dropped them into the secret compartment of his gold cigarette case.

"Tally-ho, Nicky!"

"Take care, Cecil!"

They walked lightly into the tangled jungle. Soon Carter could no longer hear Young's faint movements. Birds sang. Leaves rustled with the furtive movements of rodents. In the distance a money screeched.

Carter brushed past vegetation, hacked occasionally at vines and branches, and slowly made his way south.

He listened to the rhythm of the jungle, hearing the music of the sounds, the ratcheting of a woodpecker, one macaw calling to another, the scurrying of small animals. It was a symphony.

He hiked four miles, sometimes on trails, other times not. He walked over a rolling mountain that rimmed one side of the valley in which lay Rancho Monte Vista. He couldn't see the ranch below because of the tall trees near him, but he could see the plumes of smoke that told him the farmers were out at work clearing land. His mind was full of the symphony.

Then he heard the discordance.

The violin section was off key.

It stopped, a pocket of silence to his right.

He walked on, unsnapping the holster where he carried Wilhelmina. The hairs on the back of his neck prickled.

He continued to walk, then silently ducked behind a log-wood tree.

Listened.

Faint footsteps padded on the duff, snapping a twig.

Stopped.

Carter walked in place behind the tree, his footsteps light but still making a slight crunching sound.

The footsteps to the right resumed.

Carter saw the blackness first, the shiny black jumpsuit. Tiger Santos.

The face was intense, a handsome Latin face with a touch of Indian ancestry in the high-ridged cheekbones. He had the grace of Felicia Santos, but in him it was translated into a predatory maleness that shouted brutality.

The forested jungle grew silent.

Carter could kill him.

One shot between the eyes, clean.

But Carter wanted him for information and safe entry into Rancho Monte Vista.

Carter stepped out from the logwood tree, his Luger pointed at Tiger Santos's heart.

"Drop your rifle," Carter said. "Now!"

Santos let it fall as if from dead hands. His cold eyes narrowed into ice.

"Señor Carter," Santos said. "We meet again. But now I know who you are."

"Kick the rifle away. To your left," Carter ordered, his gazed fastened on Santos's hands.

The Nicaraguan kicked the rifle, and it slid beneath a bush.

"Turn around," Carter snapped. "Back up to me, slowly, your hands behind your waist."

Santos did as he was told, his back stiff with resistance.

Carter pulled a special nylon cord from his belt. It had the strength of steel but the lightness of cloth.

He held the loops in his mouth, the end in his hand to wrap around Santos's wrists.

Santos backed closer, his feet in the tall boots still quietly catlike.

It was a sudden movement. The split second before, Carter knew it was coming.

Santos leaped, arched backward, and hurled himself blindly at Carter.

Carter jumped away, the rope still in his teeth.

Santos's hand snagged on the Luger, knocking it from Carter's grip.

It fell with a soft *plop* onto a patch of thin grass.

Carter spun and lashed a foot at the fallen Santos.

Santos rolled and leaped to his feet, untouched and grinning evilly.

The Luger was on the ground between them.

Shoulders hunched, eyes on each other, they circled warily.

Santos had the face of a trained wild animal. It wasn't in the flesh and bone, but in the intelligence and aim. He radiated savage cleverness. And he enjoyed it more than any man should.

Slowly they circled.

Carter watched Santos's shoulders for the imperceptible dip that said Santos would drop for the Luger.

His gaze never wavering, Carter let the rope fall from his teeth to his hand.

"You are not quick enough," Santos hissed. "No one is quicker than me."

"You think too much of yourself," Carter said and smiled.

He fastened a loop in the rope as they stepped, one foot carefully after the other.

He swung the loop into a circle beside his knees.

"Go for the gun, or I'll catch you where you are," Carter said, still smiling.

Tiger Santos's gaze faltered to the gun for just a moment of uncertainty.

It was all Carter needed. Unsureness had lost more battles than poor skills ever would.

Carter's loop sailed through the air.

Santos dodged, going for the Luger.

The dodge took only seconds because Santos was indeed as quick as he claimed. But for the Killmaster, it was long enough.

Carter whisked up the Luger.

The loop fell empty to the grass.

Santos crouched on his hands and knees on the ground.

"Don't move," Carter warned him. "I want you alive, but I won't lose any sleep if I have to kill you."

Santos grunted an acknowledgement.

"Lie flat."

Reluctantly, Santos, in his shiny black jumpsuit, stretched out on the dirt. He reeked of sweat and days of not washing. His legs twitched.

"If you kick me, I'll shoot your foot," Carter said and crouched.

He waited, then wrapped the rope around Santos's ankles, knotted it, and pulled the rest of the rope up to tie the Nicaraguan's hands back together at the wrists. Once he had the hands down, he untied the ankles and flipped the rope up to Santos's neck. He tied the rope there now, so that the head was pulled back awkwardly, the rope taut to the wrists. Santos wouldn't be comfortable, but he could walk.

"Get up."

Santos rolled clumsily to his feet. His face was pinched with sullen anger. A malicious little boy with an overwhelming hunger and an empty cookie jar.

"You don't look so tough now," Carter commented and pushed the killer's ass with his foot. "Walk!"

"I will get you!" Santos growled.

"Save your threats for someone who's impressed."

Carter followed Santos down the green mountain, past occasional fields planted with maize, the corn the Maya considered the sacred gift of the gods, and into the valley below where Rancho Monte Vista spread in all her rugged glory.

Campesinos rested their hoes on their shoulders and stared with surprise at the pair. The two men walked grimly on until the soldiers that Carter knew would come surrounded them on horseback.

They pointed their rifles at Carter, not at Santos.

"For the general!" Carter shouted up at the soldiers in Spanish. "A present!"

The soldiers turned to the lieutenant who had found Carter and Tice in the rainstorm days before. He considered what to do.

"I've gambled my life coming here," Carter said. "I only want to talk to General Hiler."

"*Bueno*," the lieutenant decided at last. "Good. The general may like that. Throw your gun and backpack up here."

Carter tossed his gear to the lieutenant, who kept the Luger and handed the backpack to another soldier. The lieutenant wheeled his horse, and dust sprang into the air. In the center of the circle of snorting, pawing horses and eager riders, Carter and Santos marched to the hacienda.

FIFTEEN

General Hilario Hiler again waited for Nick Carter on the terra-cotta steps of the expansive hacienda. He held a glass of aguardiente in one hand and a dueling pistol in the other. Next to him stood bone-thin Maxim Barkov, his vulturelike face immobile as stone. There was no sign of Linda, Philip Tice, or Agrafina. The general waited for Carter to come to him. He ignored Tiger Santos.

"You killed my people," the general accused Carter.

"They were trying to kill Tice."

"They only wanted to hold him—keep him from harming my *compadre* here," the general said, gesturing with the glass at Barkov.

Carter stood at the bottom of the steps looking up. The courtyard was mostly empty. Four women washed clothes at the well. Children played in the dirt nearby. The lieutenant dismounted and carried Carter's Luger and backpack to the general. The other soldiers sat astride their mounts, watching. The general nodded at the young lieutenant to hand the equipment to Barkov.

"Come in," the general said abruptly to Carter. His patience was wearing thin. His fingers moved with agitation on the glass and pistol. "You, too, Lieutenant. With your rifle."

The general stalked into the living room, going around the

chairs to the wall that contained the bark paintings, the rubbing of the glyphs, and the rendering of the fierce Mayan warrior.

"Do you see this?" The general angrily pointed the old gun at the glyphs. "Do you know that we cannot translate these? We have no idea what they really mean. And that is because the conquistadores systematically killed all our educated people—the priests, teachers, and rulers. Then Fray Diego de Landa burned their records! The only writings left were painted inside our temples on the stone walls. But there was no one alive who could read them—or teach others to read them. So this upstart Catholic friar Landa took it upon himself to write his own version of the history of our people. The Maya go back almost four thousand years and we are left with almost nothing but what a foreigner told us! We were a great civilization while the Europeans were still rutting in roads like pigs!" The coiled-spring body of the general rocked with fury. "Do not tell me that our cause is not just! It is our destiny to unite again and rule ourselves like men!"

"That's right," Barkov said soothingly. He had a thin, feminine voice, brittle with coldness. "I'm going to untie Santos now."

"What?" the general said, pulling his fanatical gaze from the glyphs and glancing around the room.

"Carter has brought Santos to us," Barkov said. "Remember, he was on a mission for the cause."

"Good idea," the general said, staring curiously at Santos. "Your neck must hurt. What did you find out?" The general drank from his glass of potent liquor.

The KGB colonel cut the rope behind Santos, and the young man's head came forward onto his shoulders. The Nicaraguan mercenary rubbed the rope burns on his neck.

"It is just like I remembered," Santos said, twisting his head to stretch the neck muscles. "Still heavily armed. A big installation. The location is what I told you, too."

General Hiler breathed deeply, his barrel chest expanding, and he sat on his chair in front of the fireplace. He seemed to compose himself, a ferocious tropical cat resting before a fight.

"You have done well," the general said. He laid the dueling pistol on the low table before him. "Lieutenant, get Santos his cash."

"I do not want the money," Santos growled.

"You will work for the cause then?" the general asked, pleased.

"I want Carter!" Santos demanded. "He'll be my pay!"

"I have other uses for Carter," General Hiler said. "Work for us for free and you will work for good. Your reward will be the best—the knowledge that you have freed your people."

"Bullshit! I do not give a damn about your cause!" Santos took a step toward Carter. "Just give *him* to me!"

Barkov laid a hand on Santos's shoulder.

"You can't have Carter. Yet."

Santos shrugged Barkov off.

"I will wait as long as it takes," Santos said, looking at Carter.

"Don't count on it, sonny," Carter said. "You didn't do very well last time."

Santos lunged, his teeth bared.

Barkov wrapped wiry arms around Santos's chest and held him back.

Santos was so close Carter could smell his ripe breath.

"You need a bath," Carter advised. "And your teeth are rotting in your head."

The general sniffed, then laughed.

Santos growled deep in his throat and struggled to get free.

"Stop it, Carter!" Barkov rasped. "Santos, you can have Carter if we don't want him." He shook the Nicaraguan within his powerful arms. "Do you understand?"

Santos froze, then nodded.

"I will wait. He will never help you!"

"Help you with what?" Carter asked.

The KGB man released Santos. And Santos brushed past

Carter and took up a position by the front door, occasionally glancing out. He didn't like being enclosed.

"I will tell you, Señor Carter," General Hiler replied. "With pleasure. Please sit. Have a glass?"

Hiler was the gentleman *ranchero* now, a gracious host. His mood swings were so extreme that he could be a manic depressive, or simply a man with a cause he deeply believed in.

"I'd enjoy that," Carter said, keeping to the general's mood. He sat in one of the leather-covered chairs.

"Compadre?" the general said to Barkov.

"Of course," Barkov said, then left.

"Do you like the outdoor life?" Hiler asked Carter conversationally.

"I spend most of my time outside," Carter said. "It's fortunate that I enjoy it."

"Naturally we Maya must, too. We plant according to the seasons. All our gods are based on the sun, moon, and our crops. When I walk the mountains alone, I know that this is the right way to live. People in cities are in prison. I have lived there myself. They sat they enjoy it, but they know nothing else. Here we must understand the rhythms of the land and the weather. How can there be any satisfaction in closing doors and curtaining windows to hide from the glories that the gods have given us to revel in?"

"A good question," Carter said.

"I have thought about this often, particularly as I grow older," the general said. "I have decided there is nothing I can do for people who choose prison over freedom."

Barkov returned, followed by Agrafina carrying a tray with four glasses filled with the amber liquid. Behind Agrafina walked Linda, her blond hair draped over one shoulder. She wore a long white *huipile* like Agrafina's. She smiled, a goddess, at Carter. She'd changed. There was new certainty in her stride and carriage.

Carter studied her.

"You work for the general now," he said to her. "You stole my plane in Cobán and brought it back for him."

"He's my father." She shrugged. "The only father I ever knew. It was my mother's mistake not to marry him. I'm not a fool like her."

Carter watched her composed grace as she handed him a glass of aguardiente, took one for herself, and sat. She had been asked to make a choice, and her emotions had won over her intellect.

Barkov and Agrafina picked up their own glasses and joined the circle of hand-carved chairs.

"How's Tice?" Carter asked Agrafina.

"Not well," she replied, worried. "He oozes poisons from his wound."

"I've brought medicines. Keflex—a strong antibiotic. In my backpack."

"I will heal him," Agrafina said, her voice now sure.

"He may need other help as well."

Agrafina shook her head stubbornly.

"My way is better," she said. "He trusts me."

General Hiler nodded.

"The old ways are best," he said. "And it is the old ways that will give us back our freedom. My people will no longer be the prisoners of people who live in cities. My good friend Barkov has shown me how to make this happen."

Barkov allowed a small smile to play at the corners of his mouth. He rolled his glass between clawlike hands.

"Go on, Hilario," he urged.

"As Maya, we learn to use the materials at hand," the general continued, enthusiastic with his audience. "We will simply use the paranoia that so-called civilized people have learned in their prisons. They never have enough money, so they make investments in Central America. They worry that Central America will rise against them, so they send money and equipment to the forces they think most friendly. The Soviets also want Central America, to protect themselves against the United States."

"It's all crazy," Linda said, agreeing. "Everyone wants to kill everyone else."

"They kill each other and us, too," Agrafina added.

"Everyone loses," the general said, "especially us."

"And the solution?" Carter asked.

"We will have our own Mayan nation!" the general said proudly, sitting tall in his chair. "Southern Mexico and the Yucatan, Belize, Guatemala, Honduras, El Salvador, and Nicaragua. And anyone else who wants to join us. Indians from all countries will govern us. It will be a wonderful community of equals, with land and work for all!"

"Utopia, it was once called," Carter said, sipping his drink. "Yours will cause a bloodbath."

"No! We have prepared well!" the general protested. "We have a fortune in money and equipment from the Soviets and North America—the KGB *and* the CIA. The word went out today. Moscow, Havana, and Washington must withdraw their people and turn over their investments to our new country—Itzamná!"

"Or?" Carter asked.

"Or we will start World War Three!"

"No one will believe you," Carter said.

"They will believe us when they see the photographs of Soviet and U.S. equipment. The jets. The guns. They must give their answers tomorrow by ten o'clock. If they say no, we will use the U.S. jets to bomb and strafe Havana. With the Soviet planes, we will do the same to Houston and the fleet off Nicaragua that your President so conveniently sent. Russia will rush to Havana's aid. The United States and Russia will send atomic bombs to destroy each other's countries. They will kill only each other!"

"And Comrade Barkov?" Carter said, nodding at the silent KGB man.

"My chief adviser," the general explained. "He understands the importance of community."

"I'm only here to help," Barkov said. His mouth smiled, but his eyes were as empty as death.

"Your country won't appreciate your 'help,'" Carter told him.

"We've been wrong to meddle here," the KGB man announced to the room. "The United States has been wrong.'' He was the kind of man who rose to power by telling people what they wanted to hear. He had the ehtics of a piranha.

"Santos brought you information about a Cuban installation?" Carter asked.

"A good mercenary," Barkov said. "His work has been useful to us."

"I could use your help too, Carter," the general went on. "Your advice and knowledge." The general drained his glass. "In any case, you are too dangerous to be let go. It is good that you came back. Now you must look into your conscience and see the rightness of what we do—and that we shall triumph. Join us!"

Carter drank slowly. All eyes were on him. He felt their inquisitive, demanding gaze. At the door, the Indian lieutenant stood next to Tiger Santos. The lieutenant's rifle rested casually across his arm so that it could be quickly aimed and fired. He guarded Carter.

"I'll think about it," Carter said at last.

"I want your answer tomorrow," the general said and stood.

Carter nodded and got to his feet. Causes sometimes turned sane men into idiots. The Maya wouldn't get their country, and they could start a war of death and destruction that would wipe life off the planet. Carter had to find a way to stop them.

Two soldiers guarded the door and two more guarded the window to Carter's room in the hacienda at Rancho Monte Vista. He sat in the hot bath that General Hiler had again ordered for his "guest." The soldiers had watched him undress, then took his clothes, Hugo, and Pierre. Carter was left with only the clean *campesino* clothes and towel on the bed, and his most potent weapon of all: his trained mind.

He mulled over the problem, turning it around and inside out. Even a genius needed sufficient information to solve a problem.

Carter stood up and climbed out of the tub. The small room

was cool. He toweled off, noting with satisfaction that the wounds on his chest had healed, the new skin pink and healthy. He dressed, refreshed.

He had the same room that was given to him when he'd first arrived at Monte Vista with Philip Tice three days before. Its bare walls were whitewashed, the floor covered in brownish-red quarry tiles. The only furniture was a narrow cot and washstand holding a ceramic water pitcher and glass. The room had a sense of humility, as if over the generations it had housed people who cared more about what they did in the room than about what they saw on walls and furniture.

Carter opened the door.

"I want to talk to Tice," he told the guards.

They conferred in low whispers.

"You come too," Carter suggested.

They looked at one another, shrugged, and led him next door.

Tice lay unmoving on a cot shoved against the wall. His tan was gone, and freckles showed on his pasty skin. He opened feverish eyes.

"Carter?" he mumbled and looked at Agrafina who sat beside him on a chair from the living room.

She laid a slender hand across his forehead.

"*Querido*," she murmured soothingly, "my darling, he arrived today. I did not want to wake you."

"She stays with me all the time," Tice told Carter weakly while he gazed at Agrafina.

"I'd like to talk to you," Carter said. "Are you well enough?"

"He must sleep," Agrafina said. "Sleep helps to heal him."

Tice looked at Carter, struggling to focus on him.

"Leave us alone, Agrafina," Tice said, more strength in his voice now. "For just a little while."

Agrafina stared from Tice to Carter and back again. She stood.

"I will be back soon," she said and walked out the door.

The guards closed it behind her and took up stations inside the room on either side of the door. The guards weren't worried. There was no way a dying man like Tice could help Carter.

"How are you feeling?" Carter asked in English as he sat down in Agrafina's chair.

The sharp, rotting smell of infection flowed from Tice and the bed. Fever blisters bled on his lips.

"I've been better," Tice said, trying to smile.

The big man filled the bed, his heels hanging over the end, his arms limp on the narrow sides. White cotton blankets were piled on him. Still, he seemed small and shrunken, a helpless image of his former self.

Tice's teeth chattered with sudden chills. Carter pulled the blankets over Tice's arms.

"Another blanket?" Carter suggested.

"It'll pass," Tice said. "Then I'll sweat."

The CIA man was burning up with fever. Dehydrated. Probably in and out of delirium. But it was the massive infection that worried Carter most. It would kill Tice soon.

"I brought you antibiotics," Carter said.

"Where?"

"My backpack. Barkov has it."

"Can you get it?"

"Agrafina can, but she wants to heal you herself with the old ways."

Philip Tice closed his eyes and groaned.

"Señor Tice wants Señorita Hiler!" Carter told the guards. "Get her!"

That was a request they knew to obey. Once of the soldiers left, and the other raised his rifle to warn Carter not to try anything.

Carter sat back in the chair and watched Tice. The sick man mumbled to himself. His breathing was shallow.

When Agrafina returned, she rushed to the bed.

"Philip! *Querido!*"

Tice didn't open his eyes.

"I want Carter's medicines," he said feebly. "The backpack."

"You are feeling worse again?" she said. "I will get you more water. The evil spirits have returned! I will make a sacrifice, wrap it in bark paper. You will feel better. You will see!"

"Agrafina." Carter took her hand. "My medicines won't interfere with yours. Together they'll cure him."

She shook her head, stubborn belief in her eyes.

"It won't hurt to try," Carter suggested.

"I want it," Tice said. "Please, Agrafina."

Carter wiped sudden sweat from Tice's forehead. More sweat streamed down his face. Carter held up the hand glistening with Tice's sweat to Agrafina's face.

"He's on fire with fever and infection. He'll die without antibiotics."

"He is better!" she cried.

Tice lifted heavy eyelids and looked at Agrafina.

"I'm dying," Tice said, staring at her. "Dying."

She watched him, horror in her face. She turned on her heel and ran from the room.

Tice closed his eyes again, and Carter picked up a towel from the arm of the chair. He dipped it into a basin of cool water and washed Tice's face.

Agrafina returned with two large plastic bottles in her hand. Linda followed, her gaze going directly to Tice.

Carter propped the big man up, and put two tablets on his tongue and a glass of water to his lips. Tice swallowed, licked his lips, and Carter laid him back down.

Tice sighed, exhausted. He slept.

"Give him one of these every six hours," Carter told Agrafina. "Around the clock."

"*Si,*" Agrafina murmured, clasping the bottles to her breast. "*Si.*"

"There's another man," Linda said hesitantly. "The others have died . . ."

"Where?" Carter said.

The women led him from the small whitewashed room, the two soldiers trailing, to a thatch-roofed hut beyond the courtyard. The injured man lying on the mat was an Indian teenager. Seventeen, maybe eighteen. An old woman sat beside him, mending a toddler's trousers. She rose and left as soon as they entered.

The young man was delirious with fever. His face, arms, and hands were splotched red with heat. He mumbled of trees, rain, death, and a man he called White Jaguar. Carter recognized the boy.

"What is it?" he asked, kneeling beside him.

"A bullet wound through the chest," Agrafina said. "I got the bullet out."

Carter said him up, gave him Keflex and water, and laid him back down.

"Is his wound clean?"

Agrafina nodded.

"I wash his and Philip's with soap and water."

"Good." Carter stared at the boy. "He was one of those who attacked Tice and me in the jungle three days ago."

"Papa sent riders to help the survivors," Agrafina said. "Papa helps all Indians."

Carter nodded and stood.

"You've done fine work here," he told Agrafina. "If all that's wrong is infection, he and Tice will probably heal. With both of our medicines." He smiled at the young woman.

She looked into his eyes, and he saw the depths of her belief. She was a slight woman, short and willowy, but she had the soul of a giant.

Carter and the two women walked out onto the hard-packed dirt of the ranch, the two soldiers guarding Carter still behind. They passed three Indian women who worked belt looms tied to *tienda* posts. The women wove white cotton into material they would sew into clothes for their families.

Linda and Agrafina smiled at the women and waved.

"I'm sorry, Nick," Linda said as they strode back toward

the hacienda. "I have to do what I think is right. I've seen too much here of how good life can be. Papa Hiler taught me how to ride, to pay attention to the wind and stars, to live in harmony with nature. I'd forgotten all that."

"She had not been to visit since . . ." Agrafina hesitated.

"Since your father killed her mother's lover?"

"Ten years," Linda said. "But it all came back. So quickly."

"You wanted it to," Carter said as they walked. "You wanted answers from the first time I met you. You won't find the answers you can live with in a plan like Barkov's."

"You have to trust us," Linda said.

"I trust my ethics," Carter said. "That's all anyone really has."

They walked silently into the hacienda's courtyard. Tiger Santos stood on the porch, leaning against a wooden pillar next to the hitching rail where two horses were tethered. Santos smoked, watching Carter with eyes like a vulture. He paused, cigarette in midair. Nothing about him moved except the eyes that followed Carter's progress up the steps.

Agrafina went into Tice's room and closed the door.

"Would you like me to come to your room?" Linda said quietly to Carter. She stroked his unshaved cheek.

"Have you checked in with your President lately?" Carter asked.

She dropped her hand.

"Of course not," she said, stepping back. "I have nothing to say to him."

"And your mother?"

"She's on location. Filming."

Linda's small face was cold with fury. Carter had rejected not only her decision to join the general, but her offer to make love.

"I'd like some food," Carter told her. "Then I'm going to sleep."

He left her standing on the wide veranda porch. He brushed past the evil-smelling Santos and went into his room.

SIXTEEN

Nick Carter awoke to the songs of crickets outside his open window. Night had fallen, a thick blackness relieved only by an occasional star that sparkled between moving clouds. Cigarette smoke trailed into his room. One of the guards outside was smoking.

Carter stood and stretched. The events of the past week crowded into his mind. A plan was beginning to take shape.

He walked to the door.

"I want to see how Tice is doing," he told his guards.

They were new guards, but they seemed to expect Carter's request. They escorted him along the veranda to Tice's door.

Porch lights made rings of light and sent shadows against the hacienda walls and into the courtyard. The shadows moved as men strolled through the courtyard to the hacienda's double front doors. There were at least three dozen of them in green fatigues. Some had silk scarves wrapped around their necks and thrown over their shoulders. They had tanned Slavic faces. Barkov's men. The pilots for the U.S. and Soviet jets. They wore patches on their shoulders. Carter looked at the two guards on either side of him. They too now had patches of Itzamná—the reptilian face with body part crocodile, part lizard, and part snake.

Carter went into Philip Tice's room.

Tice's head was propped up on a pillow. His face was

tired, but the eyes were lively with intelligence. He held a glass of water in his hand. Signs of a reduced fever showed in the single red blotches on each cheek.

"You're back," Tice said.

"You remember." Carter smiled and sat in Agrafina's chair.

"Bits and pieces. Agrafina's been giving me the Keflex. Also chanting and doing a few other weird things."

Carter laughed.

"You're feeling better."

"Much. But I don't think I'll play football for a while."

The men grinned at one another, each glad the other was alive.

"Where's Agrafina?" Carter asked.

"Some big party the general's putting on. Guests. I don't know exactly."

"Anyone fill you in on what Itzamná is all about?"

The big man shook his head.

"Can't say I've particularly cared," he said.

Carter nodded and told Tice the details. As he talked, Tice's free hand moved over the blankets, grabbed a handful of cloth, and squeezed.

"Now I know where that million dollars disappeared to," Tice said angrily.

"Missing any equipment too?"

"Not that I know of. Navy jets! Damn!"

"Hawk will trace that one down. Meanwhile, we don't have much time to stop their plan to bomb Havana, Houston, and the fleet."

"Tomorrow! I'll be up tomorrow!"

"You've got the strength of a kitten."

They looked at the hand that grasped the blankets. It trembled with exhaustion. Tice released the blankets and sighed.

"This is a hell of a situation," he said.

"Do you know anything about White Jaguar?" Carter asked.

Tice drank from his glass and considered.

"Must be Barkov's code name among the Mayans. A couple of them called him that out by the corral during the fight."

"I thought so." Carter sat back.

"What does it mean?"

"It means that maybe I've got proof that the general's being duped."

"Agrafina?"

"Her, too. And Linda. Dreamers are important because they push for progress. But they get so hungry for the dream sometimes that they close their eyes to everything else."

Tice stared thoughtfully across the room.

"I want to stay here," he said quietly. "Marry Agrafina. She has different ways, but I think we can make it work on this land. I want to grow crops again. I want to take care of animals." He looked out the windows into the night. "This is beautiful country."

"What about love?"

"Isn't that love?"

"Of the land, not the woman. You won't do her any favor to marry her if you don't love her."

"I love her, sure!" Tice said. "She's young and beautiful. She's taken care of me. Barkov wanted to kill me. She saved me!"

The big man's face was flushed with anger. Fever came again into his eyes. He closed them weakly.

"I do love her," he said.

Carter patted his shoulder.

"We'll talk later," he said gently. "I've got to get to work."

"I understand," Tice said. He lay motionless beneath the pile of blankets.

Carter padded to the door and opened it.

He let worry flood his face.

"Come in!" he told the two guards. "Quick!"

The two Indian guards ran in and stared at Tice.

Carter closed the door.

Knocked the rifle from the last guard.

Kicked the rifle from the first.

They stood stunned at Carter's speed, then whirled, hands raised.

Carter grabbed one's wrist and flipped him over into the other guard. They sprawled, surprised, on the quarry tile floor. They were not professional soldiers.

Carter dropped to his knees and quickly pressed fingers to both men's necks. They went limp, unconscious.

"It sure took you long enough," Tice said, smiling from the bed.

"Guess I'm slowing down," Carter said and grinned back.

He grabbed the guards by their shirt collars and dragged them to the door.

"I'll take them to my room. It'll give me more time."

"Let me know what you find out," Tice said.

Carter turned out Tice's overhead light and opened the door. Two Soviet airmen stood on the porch outside the living room, drinking and smoking.

Carter waited.

The men laughed and drank their drinks.

Carter picked up one of the guards' rifles and heaved it out the door and far into the shadowy courtyard.

The airmen turned at the sound and looked at one another. They ground out their cigarettes and went to investigate.

Carter slung the other rifle across his shoulder and pulled the two guards into his dark room. He silently closed the door, and tied and gagged the unconscious men with their belts and ripped bedsheets.

The guards outside his window were smoking marijuana now. In the distance, cattled lowed and voices from the party talked and laughed.

He stood and peered out the crack of his doorway, and saw the two Soviet airmen return to the porch and walk into the living room. They carried the guard's rifle.

Carter streaked down the veranda, through the courtyard, and out into the night.

Carter found the wounded Indian boy still lying on the mat in the same hut where Carter had treated him earlier that day. But now the single room contained a family as well: father, mother, grandmother, and four young children. They were eating, and the air filled with the salty odor of fried tortillas.

"It is the white devil!" the mother exclaimed, frantically gathering her children to her.

The father stood, short and stocky. Farming had given him muscles that rippled across his shoulders and down his arms. He stepped in front of Carter.

"What do you want?" the Indian asked suspiciously.

"I came to see how your guest is feeling," Carter replied.

"The general said we were not to harm you," the farmer went on, "but I do not have to let you in."

"I gave your friend medicine. Is he better?"

"He is a stranger!" the mother said. "He is nothing to us! Señorita Agrafina only asked us to care for him."

"That man came today with the *señorita*," the old grandmother said, nodding at Carter. She gummed a tortilla nervously.

The farmer looked at the old woman, then back at Carter.

"Your guest's crazy talk should have lessened—the delirium," Carter said. "General Hiler asked me to talk to him now."

The farmer flexed his hands, undecided.

"That white devil broke Bonifacio's arm at the corral!" the mother called. "My brother won't be able to work his fields for weeks!"

"The stranger knows important information that will help the general with Itzamná," Carter explained. "You don't want to disappoint General Hiler."

The farmer looked at Carter. Carter knew about Itzamná, and the general had sent him.

The family gathered themselves together, the children

carrying their tortillas, and the family left the room.

Carter squatted beside the mat and balanced the rifle across his knees.

The young man from the jungle ambush opened his eyes and stared at Carter. His face was drawn, thin from fever and never enough food. In the usual course of events among his people, he would be married by now, and a father.

"You heard?" Carter said, feeling the boy's forehead.

"I will live?"

"*Si*." Carter smiled. "Your fever has broken."

"The fire!" the Indian sighed. "It ate my bones!"

"Why did you try to kill me and the tall blond man?"

"You come from General Hiler?" the boy wanted to know. "If you come from the general, then he knows already. You do not come from the general!" He moved restlessly on the mat and tried to sit up.

Carter pressed his shoulders down.

"Don't try it. You're still too sick," Carter said. "The general has been fooled. He didn't send you. He wants to know who did."

The boy's eyes glazed with confusion.

"I do not understand," he said.

"Tell me what happened," Carter urged gently. "Then I will tell General Hiler. He'll figure it out."

The weak young man sighed again, his body shuddering with the effort. Then he began to talk.

A half hour later, Nick Carter stood outside the hut. The farmer's family filed past Carter, staring at him, then walked back to their home. The night sky had clouded over, and no stars showed. A silver glow from the hidden moon spread low in the sky.

Carter walked back toward the hacienda. He needed a radio. Horses whinnied and pawed the dirt in the corral. Candlelight glowed in the little stores and huts. Inside, people ate their dinners and prepared for bed.

The screams came from the hut Carter had just left.
Women and children screaming.

Carter raced back.

A shadow darted from the doorway, a long knife in his hand. It dripped something onto the ground. Blood.

Still running, Carter raised the rifle and fired. As if by instinct, the runner ducked and tore around the hut.

Carter raced after him.

The man was gone.

Silently, Carter watched. Waiting for a sound. Any sound. But all he heard were the piercing screams from the hut. He returned and went in.

The two women and four children were pressed against a wall, panic on their faces. They continued to scream. The two youngest children buried their heads in their mother's skirts. The farmer leaned over the mat.

The ragged blankets had been thrown back. A river of blood poured down the sides of the Indian boy from the jungle. He had been cut from throat to testicles, a savage killing by someone who enjoyed it.

"Tiger Santos?" Carter said.

The farmer looked up, his face twisted with fury that his home had been defiled by murder. He threw the blanket up over the dead boy. Blood quickly soaked through.

"I don't know who did it!" the farmer shouted. He would rather be angry than grieve at the loss of life. That would come later, when he was alone.

The farmer picked up the ends of the mat and dragged the body out the door. A crowd of curious *campesinos* and *charros* circled the dead boy outside. The farmer ran back into the hut and hugged his family to him. He stroked the children's hair and murmured soothingly to the two women in Mayan dialect.

"Did anyone see where the killer went?" Carter asked the crowd outside.

They shook their heads and averted their eyes.

ouldn't stay. Soon soldiers would come.

rried back toward the hacienda, keeping to the outside the corrals and huts.

The shape of a sleeping *campesino* was huddled against a
cattle corral in a dark shadow. Carter slipped on past.

"In trouble again, Nicky?"

Carter whirled at the soft whisper.

"Cecil?"

He crouched, moving back to the vague form.

"You are a bad boy." Cecil Young chuckled from his
blanket. "One scrape after another."

"I've been waiting for you," Carter retorted. "Get lost?"

"Been busy, lad," the British agent said seriously. "Got
away by the feathers on my tail."

"Who's after you?"

"Cubans. A whole swarm of them out there. Led by that
beautiful Nicaraguan vixen," Young said and grinned.
"You know, Nicky, she's a bit upset with us."

Carter chuckled.

"Are they after us or the general?" he said.

"Mostly us. We've ruined our reputation with them, I'm
afraid. No one has a sense of humor these days."

Carter laughed softly.

"Can you find them again?" he said.

"What? Are you daft, lad?"

"We're going to need them," Carter explained. "Here's
what I want you to do."

As Carter crouched and talked quietly with the old agent in
the shadows next to the cattle corral, Indians ran to the
hacienda. They were followed out quickly by the mass of
Soviet airmen and a contingent of Mayan soldiers. All ran
toward the hut where the Indian boy had died, then they
spread out through the other huts, searching.

"So you think Barkov put two and two together," Young
said thoughtfully. "They traced the soldier's rifle back and
found you missing. Barkov got worried about the surviving
boy's talking."

"That's right," Carter said. "Barkov could easily calm the general—say he'd take care of finding me. Instead, he sent Santos to kill the boy before I got to him. Now Santos is out there, hoping to kill me too."

"You're in a peck of trouble, Nicky," Cecil Young said.

"You understand what I need you to do?"

"Leave it to me," the old gentleman said, rubbing his hands. "Nine A.M. sharp!"

"Good luck!" Carter said, then moved silently away around the corral.

"Same to you, lad!" Young called softly, then stood up and walked briskly away in the opposite direction.

The black night was airy with mountain breezes that rustled trees and the tops of carrots and beets planted in the kitchen garden at the back of the hacienda. Carter walked on cat feet around the turned-over plot and slid next to the kitchen door. Inside, women laughed, pots clanked, and warm food odors swept out into the cool night.

Carter walked boldly through the kitchen door.

The women shrieked and scurried away.

Carter strolled through the kitchen and into the living room. There General Hilario Hiler sat in his chair before the fireplace, staring deeply into a drink. Barkov stood at the front door. Agrafina and Linda were next to Barkov. The three gazed out into the courtyard. The room was littered with glasses and full ashtrays. A banquet table had been set in a vast alcove, the carved mahogany screens pushed back so that the lit candelabras cast a soft glow toward the electric lights of the living room.

Carter raised the rifle and checked the chamber. At the small sound, the four people turned.

"Close the door," Carter ordered, pointing the rifle at Barkov.

Barkov's bone-thin face contracted. He narrowed his eyes.

"Don't think about it," Carter warned. "Just do it!"

He walked toward Barkov with the rifle pointed at Barkov's heart. Barkov closed the door.

"You've got the idea," Carter said. "Now come over here next to the general."

The KGB man and the two women watched Carter as they slowly returned to their chairs.

"How could you, Nick!" Linda cried.

"You killed Cacimero!" Agrafina accused.

"The boy in the hut?" Carter asked, then shook his head. "Santos did that. Barkov's orders."

"And Philip?" Agrafina said bitterly. "Will you kill him, too?"

"Sit down," Carter said irritably.

He took up a position next to Barkov's chair so that he could watch the four conspirators and the front doors and back kitchen door as well.

"Hand me your gun, Barkov."

Carter touched the muzzle of his rifle to the side of Barkov's scrawny neck. Gingerly, Barkov lifted a Luger from his inside pocket and handed it to Carter. He wasn't a fool. Carter slung the rifle over his shoulder and balanced the Luger in his hand.

"Good," he said. "Now yours, General."

General Hiler pointed to the dueling pistol on the low table in front of him.

"That is all I need," the general said, his eyes smoldering with angry fire.

"Hand it to me," Carter told Barkov, pressing the muzzle of the Luger against his neck.

Barkov leaned for the pistol, the Luger's muzzle following him. He handed the pistol to Carter. Carter withdrew the Luger from Barkov's neck and rested it on his arm. He unloaded the old pistol, then threw it on the dining alcove's floor.

"My men will be back," Barkov said, rubbing his neck. "You are a dead man."

"We've got time to talk," Carter said casually. "You first, Barkov."

"You will have to be executed, of course," General Hiler announced from his chair. He gripped the arms of the chair, his knuckles white.

"Papa!" Agrafina cried. "Don't upset yourself!"

"I have nothing to say to you," Barkov growled at Carter.

"Barkov is the one who should be executed," Carter told the general. "And for reasons you don't know. Barkov obviously handles your money and equipment. Less obviously, he's responsible for killing your men."

"Carter!" Barkov reared up, claws raised to strike.

Carter batted him down. The front door opened.

"Kill him!" Barkov shouted at the door. With men and weapons, he was a giant.

Carter crouched, ready to fire.

Philip Tice walked in stiffly, his arm across the bandages on his stomach. He closed the door. His face was white with the effort.

"I heard a noise in the kitchen . . ." he said and fell into a chair.

Agrafina rushed to him and brushed the hair from his eyes.

"Don't fuss," he told her kindly. "I'm all right."

She felt his forehead and looked into his eyes. There was a sad smile on her face as she tended him. He didn't know that he loved her, and that hurt her.

"You're just in time," Carter told Tice. "I was about to describe his good friend Maxim Barkov to General Hiler."

"I'll kill you myself!" Barkov threatened.

Carter chuckled.

"Give me a gun," Tice said, looking at Barkov. "I feel naked here."

Carter handed him the rifle. The CIA man took it, held it with one hand, and put his other arm around Agrafina's shoulders. She nestled against him, and he smiled fondly down at her.

"You were saying," Tice said.

"I was saying," Carter said, "that Barkov has been posing as the general's representative with the Indians. He gave

himself the name White Jaguar and spread word that to obey
him was to obey you, General.''

"I have no objections," the general said. "He understands
what I want. What I want is what he wants!''

"He knew through his Cuban connections that I was
caught in the old Mayan cave," Carter continued. "He used
the names Itzamná and White Jaguar to order the Indians
living nearby to ambush me and Tice." Carter watched
Barkov's thin lips curl into a snarl. "Save your breath,"
Carter advised Barkov. "Then he alerted you that I was in the
area too, General, in case I escaped. Either way, he was
covered. The price of my capture was irrelevant.''

"Lies!" Barkov shouted. "All lies!''

"Mayan boys died because of that ambush," Carter went
on. "Killed by Barkov. Barkov would've killed me here
himself, but he was afraid of crossing you, General Hiler.
You wanted to convert me. He was safe as long as the
survivors you brought here from the ambush died. That's
why he ordered Santos to kill Cacimero—the savage, inde-
fensible murder of an injured boy.''

Barkov jumped to his feet.

"Capitalist murderer!" he shouted.

Philip Tice stretched out a leg and kicked Barkov's feet out
from under him. Barkov fell into the chair.

"He used the same ruse to get your soldiers to attack Tice
at the corral," Carter said. "Ask them yourself. It's not
information they would think to give you. They assumed it
was your orders.''

The Indian soldiers from the attack on Tice were alive.
They would talk to the general. And, from the look on the
general's face, Carter knew their leader would ask them.

Barkov watched General Hiler and came to the same
conclusion.

Barkov's lips stretched back over his teeth, a cornered
animal, but not yet beaten.

"You cannot stop us!" Barkov snarled. "It's too late! The
United States and Russia will cave in tomorrow morning, and

we'll have Itzamná—one of the richest countries in the world. Oil from the Reforma fields! Natural gas! Coffee! Gold! Big industries! I will make the country great! I will run it with all the Western accouterments that Central America can buy! This part of the world is used to dictators. I will be the biggest and best of all!''

''And what if the big powers don't agree?'' Carter asked.

''We will send the jets!'' Barkov shouted. ''We have nothing to lose!''

''*Basta!*'' the General said and leaped to his feet. ''Enough! I will not have Itzamná birthed in evil blood!''

''Papa!''

The massive front doors burst open.

Soviet airmen filled the doorway, guns raised.

SEVENTEEN

There is a moment before violence that stuns everyone. Attacker or attacked, surprise at what is to come stops the heart and fogs the mind. That is when training and intelligence show. Killmaster Nick Carter knew exactly what to do. He was a full fifteen seconds faster than everyone else.

Carter fired Barkov's Luger through the throat of the first Soviet airman.

Blasted the temple of the second.

Blood gushed out of the first airman's throat and soaked into his immaculate white scarf. He clutched his neck, an amazed look on his face, and collapsed as the second airman's blood, cartilage, and brains spewed into the air, a mist of pink. The second airman keeled over like a felled tree.

Shooting their guns, Barkov's men leaped over their dead comrades and scattered through the room.

Carter rolled and shot as the airmen's bullets bit into the clay tile floor, sending chips into Carter's skin. He knocked over a low mahogany table and set it on its side as a shield.

Linda crouched and ran. She picked up a rifle and skidded to Carter's side.

"Want some help?" she asked as she aimed and fired.

"You are talented," Carter said.

"What's the plan?"

"Survival. Until tomorrow morning."

He hit the arm of one of Barkov's Russians as the man moved his rifle onto Linda. The arm snapped, and the rifle fell. The airman stared in astonishment at his dangling arm.

"Stay here," Carter told Linda. "We're too big a target together."

Carter crouched and ran. The Russians had taken up positions behind chairs, tables, even a coat rack. Anything for protection. Their gunfire thundered when they saw Carter in the oper.

The coiled-spring body of General Hiler leaped onto the table in front of his chair.

"No more deaths!" he demanded.

Carter slid behind a bureau and pushed it farther from the wall.

Philip Tice got to his feet, confusion left over from his illness on his face. He weaved uncertainly, a pale giant, then seemed to gather himself. He let out a mighty roar, then swung the butt of his rifle across the backs of the heads of two of Barkov's renegade Russians.

The other airmen ignored the general and fired at Tice as he dropped behind his chair and warily edged out to return the fire.

General Hiler jumped off the table and pushed the shocked Agrafina back against the fireplace. Incensed by what he saw, he picked up a rifle from a fallen Soviet soldier.

Carter leaned out to fire. A bullet passed through his upper arm muscle, and searing pain shot to his brain.

Carter fired into the nose of his attacker. The soldier's face disappeared beneath a volcano of blood.

"You've hit Carter!" Barkov shouted. "Now kill him!"

General Hiler pushed his rifle against Barkov's chest.

"Stop them!" the general ordered, pressing the rifle into Barkov's thin rib cage. "Your Itzamná is over!" The general's face was clear with sanity . . . and relief.

"It's too late!" Barkov said. He shoved the general away. "*You're* too late!" He raised a rifle.

"No!" Agrafina screamed, her hands to her face.

Suddenly the room was silent. Smoke clouded the air. Bullet holes riddled the walls. Broken pottery, lamps and furniture littered the room. The sharp, burning smell of cordite permeated everyone and everything as the two leaders faced one another.

All watched the Mexican general and the renegade Russian KGB agent.

"This is wrong," General Hiler said, waving his rifle at the dead and injured men. "It is not our plan. We use international pressure to get our freedom. All we are doing here is killing each other." He looked slowly around the big room. "I have seen enough death to last a lifetime."

Barkov's hooded eyes flickered as he came to a decision: the general was expendable.

Carter fired at Barkov. *Click.* He was out of ammunition.

Barkov fired four bullets into General Hiler's chest. They were a tidy four holes, directly into the general's heart. Blood bubbled up and streamed down his neat fatigues.

"Papa!" Agrafina shrieked and threw herself across her father's blood-drenched chest. She tried to prop him up, but he slipped down between her arms, his features slack as the life poured out of him.

"Sorry, *compadre*," Barkov told him. "You're a liability now." He took Agrafina's arm and pulled her up from Hiler's body. "Agrafina will be better. Easier to control."

"No, you don't!" Philip Tice said, stumbling to his feet. In a sudden burst of adrenaline, the big CIA man slapped Barkov back and pressed Agrafina to his chest. He stepped toward the door. "Darling Agrafina," he crooned to her as tears streamed down her face.

Barkov shook his head, disgusted that Tice had forgotten his professionalism. Instantly he fired into Tice's back, severing the spinal cord and piercing the heart. Tice grunted and jerked. Agrafina turned, eyes wide with disbelief, as Philip Tice collapsed, dead.

Carter lunged across the room. Barkov shoved the muzzle of his rifle into Agrafina's weeping face.

"Quit, Carter," he said calmly, "or I'll kill her."

Carter stopped and breathed deeply. He made his feet stand still on the floor. Luck was with Barkov, this time. Barkov needed Agrafina to keep the Indians with him, but he'd still shoot her if he had to. To get Carter. And from the icy hatred on Barkov's face, Carter knew the Russian would sacrifice his own mother if he had to. Barkov despised any man he thought to be better than he.

Carter dropped his rifle.

"Nick?" Linda whispered.

Carter gazed at the bloodied bodies around the room. He stared at Philip Tice's motionless, crimson back. Sorrow welled inside him. The big man's sandy hair was splashed red with his own blood. His torso had fallen in an unnatural angle across Agrafina's chest and legs. What only a few moments ago had been a man full of healing, life, and love was gone forever.

"Put it down," Carter told Linda grimly.

She nodded, laid the rifle on the floor, and stood up.

From the doorway, Tiger Santos laughed as he took in the scene. He closed the door again.

"The natives outside are getting restless," he said to Barkov.

"Tell the Indians that Carter killed General Hiler and the CIA man Tice," Barkov said immediately, pleased with his quick thinking. "They'll believe that!"

"I still want Carter," Santos reminded the colonel in a deadly voice. Killing Carter would prove something he didn't believe himself—that he was a man.

"I won't forget," Barkov said. "I want him too."

Santos dipped his head in acknowledgment of his boss. Theirs was an uneasy alliance. As long as Barkov had the money and the men, Santos would obey.

"Now, my dear," Maxim Barkov said to Agrafina. He stepped back and dusted imaginary specks from his clothes as she wept. "You will do exactly as I say. As long as you do, your friends Nick Carter and Linda Stone will live. Disobey me . . . and I will let Tiger Santos have them. You and I will watch.'' He laughed softly as he pictured the torture in his mind.

Linda looked at Carter. He shrugged and smiled reassuringly at her.

''Take them away,'' Barkov ordered his airmen. ''Put them in a room and *you* guard them. No Indians this time.''

Surrounded by Barkov's renegades, Carter and Linda walked to the door.

''May I help you up, my dear?'' Barkov said to Agrafina, reaching out a hand.

As the two agents walked out the door, Agrafina's deep sobs followed them and joined the weeping of the Indians in the courtyard.

That night at Rancho Monte Vista was cold. The chill wind seeped in around the door of the hut built of timbers. High up, a single window with iron bars caught the wind. It funneled down cold on Carter and Linda where they lay huddled together beneath a thin blanket. The floor was of long wood planks that stretched unbroken the length of the prison hut, about eight feet. No one could tunnel out.

Tears ran down Linda's face. She rubbed her arm across her eyes and sobbed.

''I thought he was right,'' she said. ''Papa Hiler knew everything. He was right about my mother. She didn't love that other man. She just . . . just wanted him.''

''We all make mistakes,'' he said soothingly. ''I knew I was low on bullets. I should've checked.''

''We didn't have time!'' she wailed. ''I didn't think Barkov would kill him—and Philip, too!''

''Being an agent is a nasty business,'' Carter said. ''You learn not to trust anyone. And Barkov has no ethics. He's more dangerous than any man with a dream. Your general had a great dream.''

She nodded and sobbed into Carter's chest.

He held her warmth against him in the cold cell. Outside, their Russian guards talked, their voices muffled by the thick wooden walls. The two agents were completely surrounded, with no weapons or equipment. And the Russians were wary. They knew better than to fall for any of the Killmaster's famous tricks. Carter was worried.

Linda moved against him, her body liquid, flowing into and over him.

She lifted her face and kissed his cheek.

"You're so wonderful," she murmured. "I know you hurt."

He held her to him, feeling the painful throbbing in his other arm. The bullet had passed through. Once in the prison hut, Linda had bandaged it with a strip from her cotton *huipile*. There would be no medicine for Carter here.

He brushed her pale hair from her forehead and pressed his lips against the warm skin.

"What will happen to us now?" she wondered.

He kissed her eyes where tears were drying.

"We'll work it out," he said. "Do you know the other preparations Barkov and General Hiler made for their plan?"

"Most of them," she said thoughtfully. "If the governments say yes tomorrow morning, then there are Russians and Indians throughout Central America who will begin the transition to a centralized Itzamná government. They'll have the airports ready to ferry out foreigners, and all foreign boats and ships will be sent away. There are three big Cuban camps with tanks and trucks and gun emplacements. The Cubans are supposed to turn those over, too."

"And if the governments say no?"

Linda sighed, a shudder trembling through her light body.

"Then the jets go out," she said. "They'll bomb as the general said, and they'll strafe the Cuban installations too—put them out of commission."

"I thought so."

"It'll be a global war, won't it?" Linda asked.

"It could start one, yes."

"What will we do?" she asked, her face solemn.

"I've been asking myself the same question."

"If you're worried, then I'm terrified. I thought that you—"

"You thought that I could solve all problems instantly. Wish I could." Carter smiled ruefully. "Right now Barkov has all the cards. We need to get out so that we can steal a few for ourselves."

"There's no way to escape," Linda moaned.

"That's what worries me," Carter said.

Tension thickened the cold air of the little hut. Outside, the guards laughed, confident of their jobs and lives. They were pioneers of a new country that would make them rich. Inside, Carter and Linda held each other. The tension could drive them apart, or it could bind them together, isolated against a questionable future.

"I don't understand the world," Linda said softly. "I don't understand how good people like Papa Hiler get driven to do such crazy things."

"When we understand that, maybe it'll stop."

"Maybe we can all just be happy together."

Linda moved her head back and looked into Carter's eyes. He stared into hers, the lapis lazuli color black in the dim moonlight from the high window. He remembered the color as if he could see it now.

He kissed the eyes again, and she murmured and burrowed against him like a small fragrant animal. She kissed his neck.

"You taste like salt," she said, licking his skin. "What do I taste like?"

She lifted her lips, and he kissed her.

Her mouth throbbed. His tongue found hers. The dark cell was warmer, friendlier. She curled over him. He pulled her *huipile* down over her shoulder and kissed her throat and the warm hollow beneath. She trembled and slid a hand up under his shirt.

His lips trailed over her smooth skin, down to her breasts.

She panted, her breasts hot.

"You taste like sex," he said huskily. "As good as you did in that bathtub."

She moaned and pulled down his trousers. He slid the loose white dress from her body. She fell on him, kissing his body and caressing him in an explosive mixture of passion and fear.

He turned her over, his eyes not leaving hers, and together they rocked the world.

When the door of the cell opened, early morning light streamed in. Carter was curled around Linda, his hand holding her naked breast. The bone-thin form of Maxim Barkov stood in the doorway, his hands on his hips. He smiled without humor. He'd found just what he'd expected.

Casually, Carter pulled the blanket up to cover Linda.

She moved languidly, murmured, then opened her eyes.

"Good morning, Colonel," Carter said. "Have a good sleep?"

Linda stiffened beside him, now completely aware of the cell and Barkov. She waited.

"Not as eventful as yours," Barkov said and walked arrogantly into the hut. He was pleased. He'd found a way to be superior to a Killmaster. Barkov not only didn't need sex, he hated it. And now he could despise Carter as weak.

"A delightful night." Carter smiled.

He stood up naked in the brisk dawn air. Barkov turned his back, disgusted, and Carter dressed.

"I came to offer you a business proposition," Barkov said.

"I can't imagine what."

Carter gestured for Linda to get up and dress while Barkov's back was turned. She nodded and picked up her clothes.

"Any word on your demands yet?" Carter asked.

"We don't expect the answers for a few hours," Barkov

said, glancing over his shoulder. Carter and Linda were dressed. He turned, a small man whose flesh clung tight and hard to a wiry frame. He was dressed now in a beige tropical suit. His shoes were white patent leather. A flashy red, yellow, and blue silk scarf cascaded from his suit jacket pocket.

"What about breakfast?" Carter said.

"You're hungry. Good," Barkov said, then slipped a hand inside his jacket and pulled out Carter's gold cigarette case. Would you care for one?" he offered, opening the case.

Carter and Barkov chose cigarettes.

"Allow me," Carter said, taking the lighter from Barkov's hand. He lit the cigarettes.

"I was stationed in Los Angeles for a while," Barkov said. "An interesting city, but there were too many cars, too many restaurants, and too many tourists looking for movie stars. What a waste."

"Power is the best aphrodisiac?" Carter commented.

"The symbols are meaningless," Barkov agreed. He paced the length of the room, counting his steps. Then he paced the width. "A disgrace to end your days in a hole like this."

"It's better than selling out," Carter said.

"What is your offer?" Linda asked. Her face was bland, without expression. Her sexuality was gone, erased by will. She knew it would have no effect on Barkov.

The renegade Russian agent smiled coldly but with new respect.

"You are interested, my dear? Good." Barkov smoked. "I need someone to replace Hiler. It's very simple."

"Hiler had good relations with the United States," Carter said. "You need someone who can deal with them. A front man."

"A partner," Barkov corrected. "I'll give you a percentage. You have been an agent a long time, Carter. I know how it wears. The physical and mental exhaustion. The emotions constantly under control. Never enough time to rest, to enjoy the good things in life. Always taking orders.''

''I chose it,'' Carter said. ''It's what I wanted, what I still want.''

''I was born in the United States,'' Linda said. ''I have relatives in Texas.''

Barkov smoked and studied her thoughtfully.

''Itzamná is an idea whose time has come,'' Barkov said, addressing them both. ''The United States and Russia are tired of the chaos here, the drain on their resources. They would like a solution they can live with. A neutral country that would continue to supply them from its resources. With both a Russian *and* an American running Itzamná, they could save face and feel some assurance about the future.''

''What about the Maya?'' Carter asked. ''What will they think? Their idea is to be rid of dictators.''

''Nonsense.'' Barkov waved his cigarette in the air. ''All they want are the little things. Land, a home, work. Their glory is history.''

''Agrafina's been giving you trouble,'' Carter said.

Barkov walked to the door, then returned.

''Some,'' he admitted, ''but she will come around. Especially if you—and Linda—join us. She trusts you. She still has the Itzamná dream.''

''But you're not part of it,'' Linda said. ''I am. I want to see her.''

''Your woman has good sense,'' Barkov said. He ground the cigarette out on the wooden floor. ''If she joins me, I won't need you, Carter.'' He gestured Linda to the door. ''Think about it, Killmaster.''

It was Carter's turn to smile.

''If I refuse, you can kill me with impunity,'' Carter said. ''It's what you want anyway. What kind of partnership would that make?''

''The best,'' Barkov said. ''We each know where we stand. No illusions, just business. Think of the power we would have—ruling our own nation!''

"That's not power," Carter said. "That's self-destruction for all of us, living that inhumane way."

Barkov shrugged and followed Linda to the doorway.

"Think about it, Carter. You have an hour." He pulled the wristwatch off his arm and threw it to Carter. "Count the minutes. Then I will kill you. Myself." He laughed in his high, feminine voice, and for a moment Carter saw the unveiled hatred in Barkov's eyes. Barkov hated what he saw in Carter, a real man with deep beliefs, a man he couldn't understand, couldn't buy, and could never be. But Barkov could kill him, the eyes said, and for the Russian that was the ultimate power. Barkov nodded curtly and strode out the door.

EIGHTEEN

Nick Carter watched out the single high window of his cell as Maxim Barkov and Linda Stone walked toward the hacienda. It was eight o'clock, and the sky was already a sizzling blue as if to deny the cold front that had passed during the night. Soviet airmen walked slowly around the prison hut, their rifles resting on their arms.

Two of them stopped and looked up at Carter.

"Look!" one of them said in Russian, grinning up at Carter. "Snow White and Dopey had a baby!"

"The great Killmaster doesn't look so great behind bars!" the other said and laughed.

"You're educated enough to go see cartoons?" Carter said in Russian. "Next you'll tell me you know how to read and write!"

"He speaks Russian!" the first airman said, surprised.

"Insults work better when you speak the language," Carter commented. "Otherwise they're just the rambling inanities of a coward."

The Russians looked at one another, then glared at Carter.

"You'd better get back to work," Carter suggested. "Barkov doesn't like idlers. He can't fire them, so he kills them."

"I hope you try to escape, capitalist pig," the second guard spat. He aimed his rifle at Carter and looked through the site. "Please try to escape!"

The airmen hooted and resumed their walk around the hut.

Carter sat on the floor and looked around the small wooden cell. The walls were made of timbers, the bark old and peeling near the ceiling. Below, it had been stripped off by prisoners with too much time and not enough to do. Initials and messages in Spanish and Mayan were carved on the timbers.

Carter felt around the walls, looking for loose logs that he could pry out to make a hole. The walls were solid. He jumped on the floor planks. Also solid. He had no equipment, no way to escape on his own.

He lay down on the mat he and Linda had shared, and stared up at the ceiling. Flies crawled across the beams, then swooped down to land. He waved them away.

Outside he heard the ranch noises of animals and people at work. Children shouted at play. The day's sounds of normalcy were misleading. Jeeps and trucks rumbled across the ranch's valley. They would be carrying supplies and men, readying preparations either for war or for a new nation delivered by the United States, Russia, and Cuba.

He refused to glance at the watch. He passed the time quietly, letting his body absorb the rest that it badly needed. He waited for Linda. She was new to her work, but she was devious. If he'd capitulated to Barkov, he would have been surrounded by the Soviets at work. At least he had fewer guards here.

One of the skills a Killmaster learns is to care for his body, an important piece of equipment. In past missions, Carter had catnapped in the branches of trees, in trenches half-filled with water, and under fire waiting to do reconnaissance work. Now he willed himself to relax his tense muscles. He closed his eyes and allowed the drifting sensations of sleep to overwhelm him.

The soft *plop* of cloth hitting wood awoke him. His backpack dropped through the window. He heard Linda's voice outside, cheerfully offering coffee and rolls to the Russian guards beside the door to his prison hut.

He opened the backpack. Inside were Wilhelmina, clean socks, and a roll of what looked like striated tape. Carter laughed softly to himself, picked up the tape, and went to the window.

The guards were nowhere in sight. In the distance, the Indian villagers went about their work among the huts and *tiendas*, weaving cloth, carrying water, tending to children.

Quickly Carter wrapped tape along the tops and bottoms of the three window bars. He rubbed his nail along the tape. The iron under the tape sizzled. The hot stench of metal burned his eyes.

He pulled the bars into the room and put on his backpack, then jumped up and balanced himself on the windowsill.

Carrying Wilhelmina, he somersaulted back onto the ground and flattened himself against the hut's timbers, slipping to the edge of the wall.

Linda's head was thrown back; she was laughing at a soldier's joke.

He saw her eyes flicker in his direction, surprised. She held the reins of a horse. The three Russians were laughing with her. She laughed again.

Carter lunged. Knocked the butt of Wilhelmina against one Russian's head. Kicked the belly of a second.

Linda lashed out a foot and tripped the third airman.

Carter punched the airmen out. They would be unconscious long enough.

Carter grabbed the horse's reins and leaped into the saddle, then reached a hand down for Linda. She picked up one of the Soviet guards' rifles and mounted behind him.

As he wheeled the horse away, Indians watched in the distance, then ran for the hacienda.

"I thought I was going to have to break you out," Linda exclaimed breathlessly as they galloped toward the east mountain. "How did you get past those bars?"

"One of AXE's new inventions," Carter said and smiled. "It's nine o'clock and we've got work to do!"

They raced through the sunlight toward the green jungle. Carter turned once and saw Barkov run out of the courtyard, trailed by a swarm of Soviet airmen and Indians. They were heading toward jeeps and trucks parked nearby.

"Watch the west!" Carter said as they galloped on.

They glanced over their shoulders. Sudden firestorms shot up among the trees to the west, billowing fires that spouted orange flames and brown smoke that towered high above the jungle trees.

When Carter and Linda reached the wall of green brush that marked the beginning of the eastern jungle, they turned to ride the edge.

Barkov's posse was in an uproar. Indians peeled away on horses and in pickups toward the fires that looked as if they could spread and destroy the ranch.

"Thank God the Indians have open fields," Linda said as they rode and watched.

"Dry and wet tinder make good fire and smoke," Carter added. "Enough to scare any rancher."

The renegade Russians watched briefly as the Indians left, then they turned their vehicles to chase Carter and Linda. Barkov stood upright in the lead jeep. He held onto the windshield with one hand. The other hand waved furiously above his head as the vehicles roared off in pursuit.

Carter and Linda raced to the road that climbed the east mountain and dipped into the valley beyond.

Ahead of them on the road was a jeep loaded with crates of supplies. The Soviet driver glanced at his rearview mirror, then seemed to leap out of his seat with surprise. He lowered his head, hunched his shoulders, and the jeep put on a burst of speed.

Still galloping, Carter took Linda's rifle, aimed carefully, and fired.

The back of the driver's head exploded. He pitched forward onto the wheel, the pulpy mass of his head steering. The jeep crashed left into the thick trunk of a tree and stalled.

Carter and Linda sped toward it. Far behind them, the Soviets' jeeps and pickups sent brown dust clouds into the air. They were gaining.

Carter reined in the horse and jumped off at the jeep. The horse snorted and blew white lather off its mouth. Linda stroked its neck and leaned forward to murmur into its ear. Carter shoved the bloody driver across the seat. He started the jeep and backed it up over the road so that no other vehicles could pass. He turned it off, leaped out, and yanked spark plugs from under the hood.

He and Linda galloped on, up the winding mountain road. The jungle sun beat down, the heat creating watery mirages ahead on the dirt track. Behind them, towering flames licked the blue sky above the western mountains. When Carter and Linda reached the top of the mountain, they turned.

Barkov's men had stopped. The vehicles formed a snaking line behind the disabled jeep. Soldiers circled the jeep and finally decided to push it off the road and into the brush.

"A great idea, Nick!" Linda said and laughed as they watched Barkov.

The KGB man in his tropical suit stormed among the soldiers, pounding backs and yelling with frustration that they couldn't move the jeep faster.

"Let's see whether the Cubans were able to get over here too," Carter said and urged their horse to a gallop.

They tore down the rough road, past trees and brush and small animals ducking back into their holes. Down below, Carter could see the jets, now uncovered and gleaming in the sun. A few pilots and mechanics wandered among the planes, checking wheels and gas gauges. They were waiting for the arrival of more pilots and orders to take off on the bombing mission for Itzamná that could start a worldwide holocaust.

There were no Cubans in sight.

"What will we do?" Linda asked.

"Get to the Westwind," Carter said, his Luger ready.

They raced on in the heat of the sun. Jungle smells filled

the air. The thick foliage of trees and plants brushed their sleeves as they came out onto the valley floor.

The sentry was waiting; he had heard their horse. He'd expected jeeps and trucks. His rifle was high, aimed.

But it was another horseman who got him.

Tiger Santos, lips stretched back over his teeth, barreled out of the jungle on his horse and trampled the Russian sentry.

"Carter is mine!" he shouted as the man writhed on the road.

Santos hurled himself off his horse, wrapped his arms around Carter, and pulled him to the ground.

Bullets exploded on the road around them as Linda tried to get a clear shot.

Santos pummeled Carter with his fists, short sharp jabs that broke the skin on Carter's face and shot red-hot streaks of pain through his injured arm.

Carter leaned back fast, belted Santos in the belly, then leaped to his feet.

Santos scrambled up, his face pinched in hatred.

Carter blasted a fist to Santos's jaw.

The Nicaraguan was an intuitive fighter. He ducked, and the blow scraped along his head.

Santos kicked high but missed. He spun to face Carter again.

Carter knicked Santos's shoulder with one fist, then waited for Santos to dodge.

As predictable as night following day, the intuitive Santos dodged, and Carter smashed him square in the face.

Santos grunted, stared amazed at Carter, then crumpled into the dirt.

High on the mountain road above them, Barkov's vehicles thundered toward them.

"What are you going to do with Santos?" Linda asked. "He'll be after us again."

"He may be useful later," Carter decided.

He grabbed the reins of Santos's horse and threw them to

Linda. He heaved Santos's body over the saddle, mounted behind him, and they rode toward the planes. Alerted Soviet soldiers were running for their rifles. Soon shots rang past Carter and Linda. They leaned low over their saddles, galloping through the jets toward the Westwind.

There a line of airmen knelt, crouched in their green uniforms like a row of beetles. They fired their rifles in a continuous barrage of bullets. It was a lethal wall. To bridge it head-on meant certain death.

Carter and Linda raced into the nearby jungle. Bullets whizzed after them, ripping leaves and tearing branches. The two agents leaped off their horses into the underbrush. The sweating horses tore away, snorting in fear. Carter dragged the unconscious Santos beneath a tree and tied him there with the lariat from his saddle. The jungle foliage covered him like a green mouth. Carter took the Luger from Santos's belt. He and Linda knelt behind the bushes and peered out.

The renegade Russians had spread flat in a line, making small targets. Their eyes searched the jungle, concentrating on where Carter and Linda had ridden in.

They shot judiciously, trying to draw Carter and Linda's fire.

"There are so many of them," Linda whispered. "Do we have enough ammunition?"

"I hope so," Carter replied "Here they come!"

As Barkov's jeeps and trucks roared into the valley, three Soviet soldiers started crawling toward the jungle where Carter and Linda waited.

Carter aimed slowly, then fired.

One of the crawling soldiers shouted and grabbed his shoulder.

Linda shot, hitting another in the arm.

The Russians opened fire.

Linda cried out and bit her lip. Blood oozed from her arm. "Damn!" she breathed, looking at the arm.

They fired at the soldiers who crawled toward them at a steady pace.

"How bad is it?" Carter asked her as he fired.

Linda shook her head and almost smiled. "I'll be okay."
She fired her rifle at a soldier who crawled with his ass in the air. He fell flat, his buttocks bleeding.

Carter held up his hand. His keen ears heard twigs snap and branches rustle inside the perimeter of the jungle.

Linda looked at him. She heard the sounds too.

"Oh, hell!" she cried. "We're surrounded!"

Maxim Barkov's jeeps and trucks skidded to stops among the jets. His loyal soldiers and airmen poured out of the vehicles. They knelt and fired over the heads of their comrades, their bodies rigid with training and determination.

Linda shot at the sounds of crawling men in the jungle.

"Stop!" Carter warned her as he blasted away at the men in the clearing.

She stared at him, surprised.

"Ah, Nicky! You do have all the fun!" The voice floated to them through the leaves and branches.

"Careful, Cecil," Carter called softly.

"Cubans?" Linda wanted to know, turning to fire again at the Russians.

"You bet!" Carter said and grinned. "Reinforcements!"

The Russians filled the landing field before them, and their bullets ripped back at Carter and Linda. The jungle rocked with gunfire.

"Wouldn't have one of your fine burners on you, would you, Nicky?" Cecil Young asked as he crawled through the jungle toward Carter and Linda. His scratched faced beamed with accomplishment.

"Sorry," Carter said. "Barkov confiscated them." He looked again at the old gentleman as he knelt on the moist ground. "Where'd you get the shiner?"

Young fired and hit a distant airman in the side of the head. The old agent grinned broadly at Carter, his left eye swollen red and purple.

"A love spat, my boy," Cecil Young explained.

"He deserved it!" Felicia Santos said. "Lecherous old bastard!"

Felicia squatted beside the men, then looked curiously at Linda in her soiled white *huipile* and sandals as a dozen Cubans crept around them in the jungle and lined up low to take on the Soviet soldiers in the clearing.

"She fights with you?" Felicia asked Carter.

"She's good," Carter said.

Felicia nodded, pleased. Ignoring the bullets whining past, she shook Linda's hand and introduced herself.

"What now, Nicky?" Cecil Young asked. "We're outnumbered. Still want to follow the plan?"

"It'll work," Carter said. "We've got a trump card."

"What?" Cecil and Felicia asked in unison while Linda smiled.

"Your brother."

Felicia's eyes narrowed, and she looked around her.

"Tiger?"

Behind the group, resting under the brush so that only his bloody face showed, the tied-up Tiger Santos lay glaring at them in his filthy black jumpsuit.

Felicia drew away, lips curled.

"He'll never help us!" she said. "He's sold his soul to Barkov!"

"He doesn't have a choice," Carter said. "Here's what we'll do."

The jungle steamed with heat. Animals and birds had vanished. The Cubans and Russians continued to fire, slowly picking one another off as Carter told Cecil, Linda, and Felicia the plan.

During a lull, Felicia crawled back to Santos.

"Do you hear me, *tigre*?" she said.

He closed his eyes in disgust.

"*Tigre! Tigre!* Papa knows about the cat. He's going to whip you!"

Santos opened blazing eyes.

"Bitch!" he hissed at her.

"Good, my brother," she said. "Papa didn't believe us about the cat. He may never believe your treachery here either. But we know. You'll do as we say, or you'll *die*!" She slashed her hand across her neck and rolled her eyes.

Santos glared at her and at his former Cuban comrades who stared back hard-eyed, then shot again at the Russians.

"You'll shout to Barkov that you've killed me," Carter said, pushing his Luger against Santos's heart. "That's your part. And then you'll drag me out. Understand?"

Santos lifted his head and saw the Soviet soldiers filling the clearing.

"You are trapped!" he said. "I don't have to do a thing! Barkov will kill you himself!"

"Perhaps, little brother," Felicia Santos said, "but you'll die before you see that!"

"No one loves you here, Santos," Carter said. "If you don't do what you're told, you won't live another five minutes."

Santos looked at Carter, at Felicia, at the Cubans, and then back to Felicia. She grinned at him and stroked her rifle. Santos was suddenly a little boy backed into a corner.

"Okay," he mumbled.

"All set," Carter told the Cubans.

They passed the word down the line.

The Cubans, Felicia, Cecil, and Linda dropped flat on the ground. They quit firing. It would take a few seconds for the Russians to realize the gunfire from the jungle had stopped. The first thing they would think was that Carter and his friends were slipped away to escape through the wilderness.

Carter untied Santos, then motioned for the Nicaraguan to crawl with him to the jungle's edge. As Santos passed her, Felicia whispered to him.

"My rifle will be on your heart every second," she warned him. "One mistake, and you're dead!"

Carter saw the pain in her eyes as she spoke. Santos missed it, not that he would have cared.

Carter stretched out on his back behind a bus. On the other side were the jets and the Russians. Santos crept to Carter's shoulders. Carter held Wilhelmina close to his side where the airmen in the field wouldn't be able to see it.

The Russians stopped firing. They listened and watched worriedly. Soon they would shoot again to protect themselves as they closed in on the jungle to investigate.

"Now!" Carter commanded Santos softly.

Santos didn't move.

"If Felicia doesn't shoot you by the time I count to three, I will!" Carter snapped. "One . . ."

"Barkov!" Santos shouted across the opening. "It's me, Santos! I have killed Carter! The others have gone!"

Silence.

Through the bush, Carter watched Barkov try to decide what to do. Two soldiers turned to him, questions on their faces. He waved them off.

"Again!" Carter told Santos, fingering the Luger.

"Should I bring him out?" Santos shouted. His young face was twisted with a child's uncontrollable fury and hate.

"Yes, dammit!" Barkov yelled in return. He couldn't resist the tempting offer. "Bring him out!"

Barkov motioned to the soldiers to follow him, their rifles aimed at the jungle.

Santos picked up Carter's shoulders and dragged him into the clearing. The Cubans crawled away along the jungle's perimeter. They would try to encircle Barkov's men.

Once in the full heat of the sun, Carter started sweating. Barkov and his men closed in. Carter shut his eyes.

"How did you get him?" Barkov asked, his footsteps moving steadily near.

"Back," Santos said in a tight voice. "Straight through to the heart."

"Good man," Barkov said. Carter heard the satisfied smile in his tones.

Gunfire blasted the stillness.

"It's a trick!" Santos screamed, falling to the ground, his

arms wrapped around his head. "It's not my fault!"

Carter rolled as the Cubans fired into the group of stunned Russians. Barkov's narrow face twisted with lethal bitterness, this time directed at Santos, not at Carter.

"Traitor!" Barkov accused.

Carter dashed through the soldiers whose only thought was to protect themselves from the Cubans' accurate bullets.

"No! No! They did it! The Cubans! My sister!" Santos begged, now on his knees.

"Slime! Scum of the earth!" Barkov shouted and shot Santos straight through the heart.

As blood ran into a lake around Santos's chest, Carter leaped to the Westwind's door.

"*Tigre!*" Felicia's mournful voice rang above the gunfire.

Carter slammed the door and raced for the controls. While the Cubans and Russians fought outside, Carter started the jet and taxied it toward the runway.

Barkov chased the plane on foot, cursing, firing a rifle wildly.

Carter's turbojet soared into the hot morning air. He circled quickly over the west mountain where faint plumes of smoke marked the dying fires that the Cubans had set in plowed fields. Indians stood around the smoking earth, hoes over their shoulders as they watched the last embers die.

Carter checked his gauges and controls for the General Electric miniguns. He flew back over the landing field built on Agrafina's inheritance. Some of the Soviet pilots were warming up their jets. Others were lined up on the airstrip as first one plane and then a second flew into the air.

Carter dipped his wing, then soared over the lined-up jets. He strafed them with a continuous, revolving stream of bullets. Jet engines exploded, and fire once again shot up into the mountain air.

The two jets that had made it into flight turned and sped toward Carter. Carter saw one of the pilots. Barkov!

Carter dipped his other wing and turned, firing off it straight into the other pilot's face. The pilot fell forward, blood splattering the broken window, and the plane spiraled down. It exploded in the jungle, tall flames jutting toward the cloudless sky.

Barkov's jet passed over Carter and angled behind it, then shot into the Westwind's tail section.

Carter flew straight up, then twisted.

Barkov followed. His position was bad. The bullets streaked by Carter's windows.

Carter circled back down, then looped to the left.

Barkov sped after him, bullets peppering Carter's wings.

Carter felt his turbojet shudder. The plane couldn't take much more.

Carter dropped the nose, pulled back on the throttle, then angled sharply right.

Barkov flew past, unable to follow Carter's intricate maneuvers.

Carter swung beside the other jet and looked directly into Maxim Barkov's hate-twisted face. Perverted rage blazed from his eyes as he shot his guns at Carter.

Carter dipped his bullet-pocked wing and fired at Barkov.

Barkov pounded the window as the bullets crashed through. His shoulders and head exploded into a bloody, unrecognizable mass.

Even in death, Barkov was angry. His fist continued to pound the air where the glass had been as his jet nose-dived into a cluster of undamaged, immaculate Russian jets trying to take off.

A giant fireball shot up from the crash. The explosion rocked Carter's Westwind, and he rode the controls away from the flames.

Carter let out a long breath. He was covered with sweat. He balanced the Westwind and flew back over the airfield.

Barkov was dead, and his soldiers no longer had a leader to rally them. The men threw down their weapons and raised their hands as Cecil, Felicia, and Linda led the Cubans out from the jungle.

The guerrilla band moved the Russians into a tight knot

and picked up their guns. The triumphant fighters raised the rifles above their heads, and waved and cheered Carter. He stared down, smiling, and watched the only figure in white—Linda—as she danced victoriously on the land of the Maya. Itzamná was over.

NINETEEN

Mexico City sprawled and throbbed under a cloak of smog. Horse-drawn carts rolled in the streets among Buicks and Fiats. People with destinations strode down the sidewalks, carrying briefcases and packages. Horns honked. Friends talked. And vendors on streetcorners called their wares: "Flowers!" "Peaches!" "Avocados!" "The finest pottery in all Mexico!"

Nick Carter and Linda Stone sat at one of the tables outside the Acapulco Café near Mexico City's great square, the Zócalo. They drank Dos Equis beer and watched the bustle of the largest city in the world.

"Nothing's changed," Linda said.

"Did you think it would?" Carter smiled.

She wore a skimpy silk camisole top with narrow straps that showed her exquisite shoulders, and a short skirt to display her long legs. Her arm was bandaged in white. Her blond hair was brushed back, glossy and sleek, over her shoulders. With her big dark sunglasses and dangling gold earrings, she looked like a tourist even in her own city.

"I suppose it's like when you lose your virginity," she said. "You expect everyone to notice you're different. When they don't, you hope that at least they'll seem different to you."

"You're no longer a virgin agent."

"I suppose I'll never feel like this about it again." She had a stricken look on her young face.

"Probably not," Carter said and grinned. "There are worse things."

Carter was freshly shaved and showered, and was dressed in crisp clothes tailored to fit him. He'd had two days of regular meals and two nights of Linda. A real vacation.

"What's it like for you?" she said curiously.

"Being an agent?" he said. "Satisfying. The work is important to me."

"That's one of the reasons you're so good at it," she said with a smile. "Was your superior pleased with your report?"

"Relieved," Carter laughed. "I even called during office hours—sorry, private joke. He's code-named it White Jaguar, just to annoy the KGB."

They laughed together and drank their beers. The air smelled of tacos, tortillas, fried shrimp, and fried pork skins. A waiter carried a tray to a nearby table. He set down tall sherbet glasses filled with fruit ices.

"Where do you suppose they are?" Linda asked, looking up and down the sidewalk.

"They'll come when they're ready."

Linda nodded, and her gold earrings jingled.

"I love the Zócalo," she said. Her gaze moved across the great square. "When I was a little girl, the buildings around here seemed like magic. They're so beautiful, so intricately designed and painted. But they're suspended on the ooze of an old lake—Lake Texcoco. See how they're tilted and sinking? They could fall over any minute, those big buildings. But they never do." Her voice was childlike, filled with awe. "I thought people were as reliable."

"You're a real tough agent," Carter said, amused.

"I will be!" she declared. "I won't make the same mistake I did at Monte Vista. I'll never let personal feelings interfere with my work again."

"Good girl," Carter said and reached across the table to hold her hand.

"Do you think Agrafina will be all right?" She looked at him.

"She's where she wants to be, living the life she loves. That's all any of us can ask."

"But her father's gone . . . and Philip."

Her hand was small and long-fingered. She wore three rings—an emerald, a filigreed gold band, and a ruby—two on the right hand and one on the left. He held both hands in his.

"Agrafina knows Philip loved her," Carter said. "That helps."

"He sacrificed himself," Linda said softly, looking at her hands and then up at Carter. "I'll miss you."

"You have your work now," he said.

"Will it be enough?"

"It has to be."

She wore a perfume so light that he could only catch whiffs of it. It was as subtle as she, and as changing.

"You have the Barkovs of the world to stop now," Carter went on gently. "As long as there are people, there'll be renegades and scavengers who live off others. Some will grow so powerful that they'll threaten our civilized way of life. Your job is to help stop them."

"That's a lot for just one person."

"You're not alone," Carter said. He lifted her small hands, unfolded them, and kissed the palms. "I'll miss you too," he said. "Very much."

"Cheerio, children!" Cecil Young called.

Carter and Linda smiled at each other and looked up.

"Been waiting long?" the British agent said. "We've had quite a day!"

He and Felicia Santos strode toward Carter and Linda's table.

"He buys me *everything*!" Felicia said gaily. She deposited an armload of bundles beside her chair, then sat down and fanned herself with her hand. "Clothes, toys, books! For the children!"

"Arab oil money," Cecil said modestly as he sat beside Felicia with even more bundles.

She looked at Carter and Linda.

"We've come too early," she announced. "They still want to be alone."

"They've been alone enough," Cecil said. He pulled Felicia to him and kissed her mouth. She leaned into him. "We want to be alone too!" he said.

The quartet laughed, full of the joy of their successful mission and the past two days of leisure. Carter waved for the waiter to bring menus. As the sun filtered through overhanging pepper trees onto the patio, they ordered their farewell lunch. They talked and told jokes, and Nick Carter felt a familiar stirring along his shoulder blades. He watched the streets and sidewalks pulse with people, old and young, poorly and elegantly dressed, with faces showing good and evil. Any one of them could be his next assignment; any one of them could want to kill him.

DON'T MISS THE NEXT NEW NICK CARTER SPY THRILLER

SAN JUAN INFERNO

Josh Billings was leading the merry-go-round check of the villa. He'd just passed the east wall and was heeling to port for a northerly sweep when he saw something fall from near the top of the wall and plunge into the jungle below.

That "something" hanging there beside Nick Carter had puzzled him from the moment the attack force had arrived to blast the laboratories and rake the compound with the chattering fifties.

When Billings had seen Carter crawl to the top of the wall, he'd hovered his craft, watching the dark villa and compound. He'd seen the twin blasts of gunfire from the villa window, seen the thing beside Carter fall into the jungle.

And he knew. Carter had found someone, a friendly, or he'd taken a captive. And now the guy was pinned down by a killing fire.

Billings checked his weapons. He had no rockets left. He'd dropped all his firebombs. But the starboard 50 caliber and the nose-mounted 20mm were still armed and ready. He decided on the 20mm.

"A-Force Three, A-Force Two," he said into the microphone. "All eyes on lookout for stragglers. Renegades in the window are mine."

He revved the engines, felt the biting torque of the swirling blades and eased the big Bell Cobra into a neat dive. He came in low, virtually on a collision course with Carter who was clinging to the side of the wall, near the top.

Fifty yards shy of the wall, he raised the chopper, topped the wall by mere inches and squeezed the red button on the cyclic pitch stick.

The chopper seemed to buck and stand still in the air as the 20mm shell burst from the cannon mounted in the nose. The pilot's eyes trailed the whizzing, sizzling shell, waited for the telltale ball of fire to burst from the offending window, then went into a power climb high over the villa.

By the time he'd circled back, Carter was walking across the compound toward the burning villa.

He gave the man from Washington five minutes to assure that the job had been done right, then hovered over the agreed parallel and lowered the hook and cable.

Carter dashed from a dark doorway of the villa and leaped aboard the hook. Billings started the winch motor and brought the warrior into the flagship.

At precisely 2:46 point ten, Carter was in the copilot's seat and the three choppers were screaming toward the bivouac area.

The laboratories had been destroyed. There were no survivors on the mountaintop. There was no leaking radiation. It had been a perfect strike, from a logistical standpoint. But the Killmaster seemed defeated, subdued.

"Who was the guy?" Billings asked as he took a 260 bearing for the bivouac area. "The guy who fell?"

"I never got his name," Carter said, his voice low, growling. "He was just a kid. Brainwashed. I could have turned him around."

"You can't save 'em all."

"I can damned well try," Carter spat.

"Yeah, guess you can do that. What next? You got any ideas on how we can hit that downtown building? The one with the A-bomb?"

Carter stared at the pilot. The silence, except for the eternal throbbing of the engine and flailing of the blades, was almost deafening.

"I have an idea," he said. "It involves putting the lives of good people on the line."

"I guess it always does."

"I'm going to use Irena," he told Billings. "I'm going to use her and probably get her killed. Also myself. Also a lot of people in San Juan."

Carter pressed his heavy shoulders into the backrest. He flashed a quick grin at the pilot, then stared glumly at the moonlit jungle below.

"That boy's death hit hard, didn't it?" Billings said.

"There were a lot of boys up there. And a grand old lady near Alto Trujillo."

"Sure," Billings said in a low, soft voice. "It's eulogy time, right?"

"No, just time for human compassion," Carter said, arching an eyebrow at the pilot.

And, Carter thought as he gazed at clouds scudding past a fast-dropping moon, it may be time to finish the job.

"I never thought soldiers took time out for compassion in the middle of a war," Josh Billings said.

Carter looked at him. "So now you're an expert on war?"

The captain grinned and shook his head. "No expert, sir, but I do believe I've learned a bit about it in the past couple of days."

"I suppose you have. When it gets right down to it, war is a simple thing of killing or being killed. Whatever, Captain Josh Billings, newly ordained warrior, get this crate moving. We have to put the lives of some good people on the line."

Billings twisted the throttle to its highest notch, smiled at the man from Washington and listened to the ear-splitting roar of the engine. Carter watched the night and thought of Irena, of his doubts about her. There was nothing to do but use her, and use her ruthlessly.

—From *San Juan Inferno*
A New Nick Carter Spy Thriller
From Charter in December